HANDSOME RANCHER

Handsome Devils Book 1

LORI WILDE
LIZ ALVIN

A s she studied him, standing near the entrance to the city council room, Megan Kendall couldn't help thinking what a handsome devil Chase Barrett was.

Everyone in the small town of Honey, Texas, thought so as well. With his drop-dead gorgeous looks and his handsome-devil smile, women fell for him like pine trees knocked down by a powerful tornado.

Even Megan couldn't claim to be immune. She and Chase had been good friends for over twenty years, and he still didn't know she was madly in love with him.

Yep, he was a handsome devil all right.

"Picture him naked," Leigh Barrett whispered to Megan.

Stunned, Megan turned to stare at Chase's younger sister. "Excuse me?"

Thankfully, Leigh nodded toward the front of the room instead of in her brother's direction. "The mayor.

When you're giving your presentation, if you get nervous, picture him naked."

Megan slipped her glasses down her nose and studied Earl Guthrie, the seventy-three-year-old mayor of Honey. When Earl caught her gaze, he gave Megan a benign, vague smile.

"I don't think so," Megan said to Leigh. "I prefer to think of Earl as fully clothed."

Leigh giggled. "Okay, maybe that wasn't such a hot idea after all. Let me see if I can find someone else for you to think of naked."

"That's not necessary. I'm not nervous." Megan flipped through her index cards.

Her argument was flawless, her plan foolproof. She had nothing to be nervous about. Besides, as the head librarian of the Honey Library, she knew every person in the room. This presentation would be a snap.

But with puppy-like enthusiasm, Leigh had already stood and was looking around. She hadn't spotted her oldest brother yet, but Megan knew it was only a matter of time before she did.

"Leigh, I'm fine," Megan tried, but Leigh finally saw Chase and yelled at him to come over and join them.

Chase made his way through the crowded room. The city council meetings usually drew a big audience, but Megan was happy to see even more people than usual had turned out to listen to her presentation of fundraiser ideas for new playground equipment.

When Chase got even with Megan and Leigh, he leaned across Megan to ruffle his sister's dark hair. Then he dropped into the folding chair next to Megan and winked at her. "Ladies, how are you tonight?"

Megan tried to keep her expression pleasant, but it wasn't easy. Ever since she'd moved back to Honey last year, pretending her feelings for Chase were platonic was proving harder and harder. At six-two, with deep black hair and even deeper blue eyes, he made her heart race and her palms sweat.

"Don't ruffle my hair, bozo." Leigh huffed at Megan's right, smoothing her hair. "I'm in college. I'm too old to have my hair ruffled."

To Megan's left, Chase chuckled. "Squirt, you're never going to be too old for me to ruffle your hair. When you're eighty, I'm going to totter up to you and do it."

"You and what orderly?" Leigh teased. "And just for the record, I like Nathan and Trent much better than I like you."

"Oh, please." Megan rolled her eyes at that one. Leigh loved all of her brothers, but everyone knew Chase was her favorite. When she was home from college, she always stayed with Chase.

"I love you, too, squirt," Chase said, not rising to his sister's taunt. Instead, he nudged Megan. "You okay?"

"I told her to imagine the mayor naked if she got nervous, but she doesn't want to do that," Leigh supplied.

"I can see why not," Chase said. "Earl's not exactly stud-muffin material."

"Oooh, I know what she should do." Leigh practically bounced in her chair. "Megan, if you get nervous, picture Chase naked."

Megan froze and willed herself to stay calm. The absolute last thing she wanted to think about was Chase naked. Okay, maybe she did want to think of him naked, but not right now. Not right before she had to speak in front of a large portion of the entire town.

"I don't think so," Megan muttered, shooting a glare at Leigh.

The younger woman knew how Megan felt about her brother, and this was simply one more not-so-subtle attempt to get the two of them together. In the past few months, Leigh's matchmaking maneuvers had grown more extreme.

"I don't think I'll need to picture anyone naked," Megan stated.

On her other side, Chase offered, "Well, if you get flustered and it will make things easier for you, you go ahead and think of me naked, Megan. Whatever I can do to help."

Megan knew Chase was teasing her, but suddenly she realized how many years she'd wasted waiting for him to take her seriously.

She'd fallen for him when she'd moved to town at eight. Dreamed about him since she'd turned sixteen. And tried like the dickens to forget him when she'd been away at college and then later working at a library in Dallas for five years.

But nothing had helped. Not even seriously dating a man in Dallas had helped. In her soul, Megan believed she and Chase were meant to be together.

If only she could get him to notice her.

"Hey there, Chase," a smooth, feline voice fairly purred over their shoulders. "You're looking yummy. Like an especially luscious dessert, and I positively love dessert."

Oh, great. Megan glanced behind her. Janet Defries. Just what she needed tonight.

Chase smiled at the woman half leaning on his chair. "Hey, Janet. Do you plan on helping Megan with her committee?"

From the look on Janet's face, the only thing she planned on helping herself to was Chase, served on a platter.

She leaned toward Chase, the position no doubt deliberate since a generous amount of cleavage was exposed. "Are you going to help with this committee, Chase? Because if you are, I might be able to pry free a few hours."

Yeah, right. Megan shared a glance with Leigh. They both knew Janet would no more help with the committee than dogs would sing.

"I'd like to help, but it's a busy time on the ranch," Chase said.

"Shame." Janet slipped into the chair directly behind him. "I think you and I should figure out a way to spend some quality time together."

Her message couldn't have been clearer if she'd plastered it on a billboard. Megan hated herself for wanting to know, but she couldn't not look. She turned to see what Chase's reaction was to the woman's blatant come-on.

Mild interest. Megan repressed a sigh. Of course. Janet was exactly the type of woman Chase favored. One with a high-octane body and zero interest in a lasting relationship.

"Maybe we'll figure it out one of these days," Chase said, and Megan felt her temperature climb.

Okay, so she didn't have a drawer at home full of D-cups, but Megan knew she could make Chase happy. She could make him believe in love again.

If the dimwit would give her the chance.

Janet placed one hand on Chase's arm and licked her lips. "Well, you hurry up, else I might decide to go after Nathan or Trent instead. You're not the only handsome fella in your family."

Chase chuckled as he faced forward in his chair once again. "I sure am being threatened with my brothers tonight. But I'd like to point out that neither of them stopped by to lend their support, and I'm sitting here like an angel."

Leigh snorted. "Angel? You? Give me a break. You could make the devil himself blush, Chase Barrett."

Chase's grin was pure male satisfaction. "I do my best."

As Megan knew only too well. She'd watched him beguile a large percentage of the females in this part of Texas. Why couldn't he throw a little of that wickedness her way? Just once, she'd like to show him how combustible they could be together.

But even though she'd been back in Honey for almost a year, the man still treated her like a teenager. She'd just celebrated her twenty-ninth birthday. She wasn't a sheltered virgin with fairy-tale dreams of romance. She was a flesh and blood woman who knew what she wanted out of life.

She wanted Chase.

After a great deal of commotion getting the micro-phone to the right level, the mayor finally started the meeting. Within a few minutes, it was time for her presentation. Megan stood, adjusting her glasses.

"Remember, picture Chase naked if you get nervous," Leigh whispered but not very softly.

Megan was in the process of scooting past Chase, who had stood to let her by. She froze, standing directly in front of the man who consumed her dreams and starred in her fantasies.

He grinned.

"You know, I think I just may do that," Megan said. "And if he gets nervous, he can picture me naked, too."

⚜

HAD TO BE THE HEAT, CHASE DECIDED AS HE SETTLED back in the wobbly folding chair. Or maybe the water. Either way, something was weird because Megan Kendall had just flirted with him.

Leigh moved over to sit in the chair next to Chase. "You talk to Nathan or Trent today?"

Chase glanced at Megan, who was straightening her notes, so he had a couple of seconds to answer his sister. "Nathan and all of his employees are working overtime trying to get that computer program done. Trent has a new officer who joined the force today, so he's busy, too. You're stuck with me."

Rather than looking upset, Leigh's expression was downright blissful. "Megan and I are thrilled you're here."

Through narrowed eyes, Chase studied his sister. She was up to something as sure as the sun rose in the east, and he'd bet his prize bull it had something to do with him breaking up her necking session with Billy Joe Tate last night.

"Whatever you're doing, stop it," Chase told her. "It won't work."

Leigh fluttered her eyelashes at him, feigning inno-cence. "Who, me? I'm not up to anything. How could I be with you and Nathan and Trent on me every second of every day? I'm almost twenty-two, Chase."

"Spare me the melodrama. Just because I don't want my baby sister having wild sex in a classic Trans Am in front of my house doesn't make me a meddler."

Leigh snorted loud enough to make some of the ladies in the row in front of them turn to see what was happening. But Leigh, as usual, ignored everyone around her and barreled on.

"If it were up to my brothers, I'd still be a virgin," she actually hissed at him. "Thank goodness I decided to go away for college. No one in Austin has ever heard of the Barrett brothers."

Chase opened his mouth to say something but ended up gaping at his sister like a dead fish. He was still formulating what to say to Leigh's pronouncement when Megan started her presentation.

Good manners, drilled into him over the years, forced him to remain silent and listen to the speaker. But what in the blue bejesus was up with the women tonight? And why was he the lucky man who got to be trapped in the middle of it?

And since when wasn't Leigh a virgin? He glanced at his sister, who was nodding and smiling at Megan as she went over the reasons why the city park needed new playground equipment.

He had to face facts. Their father had run off with a waitress when Leigh had been four. Their mother had died when Leigh had been eleven. She'd been raised by three older brothers who might have been strict with her but who did a fair amount of hell-raising on their own.

He should count his lucky stars that Leigh hadn't made him an uncle already.

But for crying out loud. He was all for liberated women, but did they all have to liberate themselves in front of him at the same time?

He turned away from Leigh, but not before making a mental note to talk to her once more about safe sex and nice boys.

Behind him, Chase could actually feel Janet Defries staring at the back of his head. No doubt she was planning all the things she could do to him if she had plastic wrap and an economy jar of mayonnaise.

And then there was Megan. Frowning, he looked at her. She was carefully explaining how the city could build a large play castle like so many bigger cities had if they raised enough money and had enough volunteers.

Her talk was going well, as expected, but Chase could tell she was nervous. They'd been friends for so long, he recognized the signs.

He gave her an encouraging smile.

And the look she gave back scorched him. Good Lord. She was picturing him naked.

Before he could stop himself, before he could even think about how downright stupid it was, he found himself picturing Megan naked, too.

And really, really liking what he pictured. Sure, a few

times over the years, he'd turned the idea of Megan over in his mind. After all, she was attractive in a sedate sort of way.

She had long ash-blond hair, pretty green eyes, and a slim body with just enough curves to keep a man interested. Sweet curves that would be soft to the touch, and silky to the taste and—

Whoa. What in the blazes was he doing? Megan Kendall was one of his best friends, not to mention a woman who actually believed in things like love and marriage. He blinked and mentally tossed a thick, woolen blanket over Megan's naked body. That would be the end of that.

"I think Chase should co-chair the committee with Megan," Leigh announced, bringing Chase's attention back to the meeting going on around him.

He glared at Leigh. "What? I don't have time to co-chair a committee." He glanced at the city council, the mayor, and finally, at Megan. "Sorry. I'm too busy at the moment."

"Everyone is busy," Earl said. "But you make time for something as important as this." The mayor leaned forward. "Don't you want your children to have a nice park to play in someday, Chase?"

"I don't have any children, Earl, and I don't plan on having any."

He looked at Megan, whose expression could only be called sad. Great. Just great. Now he'd disappointed her by saying he wouldn't co-chair the committee. Well, at least he'd found a way to get her to stop picturing him naked.

"Hold on a minute here," Leigh said. "It's your turn

to help, Chase Barrett. Trent's the chief of police, so he does a lot for this town. And Nathan's computer company supports practically everybody. I've volunteered at the senior center, and I'm coming back to town next fall to do my student teaching. It's your turn to do something to help."

A slow, steady throbbing sensation started somewhere in the back of Chase's brain. Leave it to his sister to put him in an awkward position. "I don't have the time right now, Leigh. I'll be happy to make a donation, though."

Megan's expression softened. She forgave him. He knew she forgave him. Naturally, sweet Megan would understand.

Dang it. Now he felt lower than a rattlesnake's rump.

"What would it involve?" he half groaned, wanting to do whatever it took to get out of this room and away from these women.

"It wouldn't be much," Megan told him. "Just help with the carnival and the auction. I'd only need a couple hours of your time for the next few weeks."

Like he believed that. A carnival and an auction sounded like a lot of work. "Why do we have to have both?"

Leigh thwacked him on the arm. "Weren't you listening? Megan explained that the carnival will bring in the people, then the auction will bring in the big money."

Chase frowned at his sister. "Oh."

"I'll be willing to help on this committee if Chase is co-chair," Janet said from over his shoulder.

The throbbing in the back of his head grew more intense as several other single women in the room also agreed to help on the committee, that is of course, "if he did, too."

"See there, Chase, you're a popular guy. Lots of folks want to help out if you join in," Earl said. He glanced at the members of the city council. "I think this sounds like a great plan. Let's take a vote."

Chase wasn't surprised the council agreed with the mayor. What wasn't to like? Everyone was happy except for him.

"I never agreed to help," he pointed out to Leigh after Megan gathered her things and headed back to sit down.

"Oh, let it go, Chase. You're like a neutered hound dog, going on about something that's long gone," Leigh said.

A soft, sexy, feminine laugh floated around him, raising his body temperature. Who in the world... He turned, bumping right into Megan. The smile she gave him was so very unlike the Megan he'd known for years and years.

Her smile was pure seduction.

"Trust me, Chase is nothing like a neutered hound dog," she said softly.

The water. Something was definitely wrong with the water in this town.

2

Chase was upset with her, but Megan couldn't muster the guilt to feel badly about how things had turned out. Chase was co-chairing the committee with her, and she couldn't be happier.

Turning her compact car onto the long gravel driveway leading to Chase's house, Megan found herself humming. Last night couldn't have gone better if she'd choreographed it.

Everyone had taken it for granted that Chase was the co-chair. Then Leigh had invited her to join the family for the traditional Sunday barbecue, and Megan had quickly accepted, leaving the meeting before Chase could finagle his way out of helping.

Now all she had to do was take advantage of this opportunity that Leigh and the citizens of Honey had inadvertently given her. Well, maybe that the citizens of Honey had inadvertently given her. Megan was fairly certain Leigh had pushed her together with Chase on purpose.

Either way, it didn't matter. She had a chance to make Chase notice her, and she planned on using that chance.

Last night, she'd stayed up late skimming two of the recent additions to the Honey Library: *Squash the Wimp Within* and the sequel, *Do It or Die Sorry*.

According to the books, many women didn't go after what they wanted in life. They had been raised to be polite, to not rock the boat. Megan knew that up until now, she had been one of those women. But no more. She'd tried being subtle, and Chase hadn't caught on.

Drastic action became her only recourse.

Getting Chase interested wouldn't be easy. With a string of broken relationships behind him, the man didn't believe in love. He'd once told her he had a better chance of Santa shimmying down his chimney than of finding a woman to love forever.

But even with his attitude, Megan would never forgive herself if she didn't at least try. In her heart, she knew Chase was the right man for her. Sure, he could be mule-headed at times, but as everyone knew, the course of true love never did flow smoothly.

Megan parked her car next to Nathan's expensive sedan and Trent's squad car and climbed out. As she headed up the steps to the front door of the white, two-story house, the Texas sun was warm on her back, even though it was only late March. But thankfully, her new cotton dress was cool.

And bright. A bright vibrant emerald-green. After a great deal of thought, she'd decided to further shake up Chase by changing her style. Not so much her clothing choices, but rather their colors.

Traditionally, Megan favored flowing dresses in calming pastels. Instinctively she knew the best way to get Chase to notice her wasn't to appear suddenly wearing a sequined bustier and spandex shorts. That kind of radical change would signal to Chase that something was up, and he'd be on guard.

But if instead she made small, subtle changes, then he'd notice her without knowing why he was noticing. She understood Chase needed time to adjust to the change in their relationship, so she wouldn't rush him. But she had hope. Lots of hope.

Because at least once last night, she knew for a fact he'd pictured her naked.

What a wonderful way to set a plan in motion. Smoothing the skirt of her sundress, Megan started to knock. Abruptly the door flew open, Leigh grabbed her arm, then tugged her inside.

"Don't let him wiggle out of this," Leigh whispered with a grin. "He's trying. But you stand firm."

Megan's spirits sank a tad. "Is he unhappy?"

Leigh huffed. "He's fine. Now head on out back. He's barbecuing dinner. Flatter his fragile male ego. I know, tell him how much you appreciate him helping, and that you think he's a great guy."

"I do. Very much. I really think this playground will be terrific for the children of Honey. Did you know the equipment there is almost forty years old? I couldn't—"

Leigh rolled her eyes. "You're preaching to the choir, Megan. And don't worry about Chase. Working on this carnival will be good for him. He'll spend some time away from the ranch, which he needs, and he'll do something terrific for the kids of this town." She nudged Megan farther inside the house. "Now, no wavering. Go outside and ask him if he needs any help with the grill."

As Megan was about to head toward the back of the house, Leigh grabbed her arm once again.

"Oh, and don't ask for any water. He keeps muttering about there being something wrong with it."

Perplexed, Megan simply nodded, then followed Leigh through the living room, past the kitchen, and into the family room. Funny, there was nothing wrong with her water.

Nathan, Trent, and a red-haired woman Megan didn't recognize sat watching a basketball game on the wide-screen TV. When Leigh and Megan walked in, the conversation floundered to a halt.

"Megan, you know my brothers. And this is Sandi, with an *i*," Leigh said hurriedly. "Trent's date."

Megan moved forward to shake Sandi's hand. The young woman was very pretty, but all of Trent's dates were pretty.

"Nice to meet you, Sandi," she said.

Sandi grinned. "Thanks. I'm really glad to be here."

Megan decided she liked Sandi with an *i* even if she knew she'd only meet her this once. Trent's girlfriends didn't last as long as a gallon of milk.

"Hi, Nathan. Trent," Megan said.

Nathan stood. "Hello, Megan. It's good to see you again. You're looking lovely today."

Megan smiled. Nathan was a natural-born charmer. He could convince birds to give up their feathers in the dead of winter. "It's good to see you, too, Nathan. I hope you don't mind me being here."

Nathan grinned, making his handsome face even more appealing. Like all the Barrett men, he had black hair and the most amazing blue eyes.

Unlike his brothers, though, Nathan's hair was styled, giving him a more polished, sophisticated look. "Not at all. I'm happy you can join us."

Trent also stood, and the grin he flashed Megan was pure flirt. "Hey, Megan. Like Nathan said, you look good today."

The way he said *good* dripped with innuendo, but since she'd grown up around Trent, Megan didn't take his flirting seriously. She merely shook her head at him.

"Cut it out, you dweebs," Leigh said. She gave Megan a little push toward the door leading to the back porch. "Ignore them. Go say hello to Chase. You two need to start planning for the carnival. That's going to take a lot of work."

"I understand you're going to have an auction as well," Nathan said. "Barrett Software will be happy to donate a laptop."

"Thanks, I really appre—"

Leigh grabbed Megan's arm once more and started dragging her toward the door leading out to the patio.

"Yeah, yeah. Nathan's the salt of the earth," Leigh said. "Now go talk to Chase."

Megan refused to budge. "Leigh, give me a second here." When she looked back at Trent and Nathan, they both had knowing expressions on their faces.

They smelled a plot.

Trent was the first to break the silence.

"Oh, yeah, Megan, why don't you go say hi to Chase? I know he'll be happy to see you."

"I agree. Great idea," Nathan said, his expression way too innocent to be believable.

Megan rolled her eyes. "It's not what you think."

But since it was exactly what they thought, she didn't see the point in saying anything else. Megan realized that everyone in the room now knew with utter certainty why Chase had been coerced into co-chairing the playground committee.

Okay, so maybe Sandi didn't know. Yet. But she probably would before dinner was over. Eventually everyone would know.

Except, with any luck, not Chase. Megan wanted to find a way to get the message across to him on her own. Slowly. So he'd have time to adjust to the idea of them becoming more than friends. With care and finesse and—

"Now I get it," Sandi announced loudly. "She has the hots for your older brother, right?"

Megan groaned. Or more than likely, he'd know in about a minute and a half.

✦

CHASE FIDDLED WITH THE STEAKS ON THE BARBECUE grill. Dinner would be ready soon, and judging from the commotion he could hear going on in the family room, Megan had arrived.

Good. He needed to talk to her. He'd come to a few decisions last night, not the least of which was that he didn't have time to co-chair any committee, even one she was running. Megan would have to accept his decision.

Once he cleared up that misunderstanding, they next needed to talk about had happened between them. He wanted to make certain she'd been kidding last night when she'd openly flirted with him.

Megan, of all people, knew how he felt about love and romance. She also knew how he felt about her. They were friends. Good friends. And even though they'd both changed a lot during those years when she'd been away at college and then working in Dallas, they'd remained friends.

Just as they'd been since that day when she'd been eight and was being tormented by a bully for being the new kid. He'd stepped in to help her, and they'd been friends ever since. Even though he was five years older than she was, Megan had always understood him without getting all sappy and girlie.

So he knew they could clear up last night's misunderstanding without any problems. There wasn't anything the two of them couldn't talk about. Even if she had developed a little crush on him, they could work through it.

He'd help her see that what she thought was love was only her hormones acting up. Naturally, they couldn't do anything about those hormones because having sex would ruin their friendship. But at least she'd know he cared.

After that, they'd simply ignore this bump in the road of their friendship. Then in a few weeks, everything would go back to normal.

When he heard the door behind him open, he glanced over his shoulder. It was Megan, so he turned toward her. "Hey."

"Hi, Chase." She sat in one of the wrought-iron patio chairs near the grill. "How are you?"

Okay. So far, so good. She wasn't flirting. "I'm fine," he said carefully, still uncertain of the waters. "And you?"

She smiled up at him, and he couldn't help noticing that her dress did really remarkable things to her eyes. Since she wasn't wearing the glasses she wore when reading, he could see her eyes clearly. They looked deep green and so incredibly inviting.

Whoa. Rein that horse in. What in the world was he doing? He didn't care if her eyes looked really green. That wasn't what they needed to talk about.

He returned his focus to the problem at hand. "Look, Megan, about last night—"

"Thanks again for volunteering to help," she said, crossing her legs. The mild spring breeze fluttered her skirt around her calves, and Chase's gaze strayed and stayed. Megan had really great legs. Long, slender. Sexy.

Oh, for crying out loud. He blew out a disgusted breath, and Megan frowned at him.

"What's wrong with you today?" she asked.

"What's wrong with me?"

"Yes. You." She smiled. "Are you truly upset about last night? I know you got railroaded into helping. But I do appreciate it, and I'll make certain you're not asked to do too much."

The sizzle of the steaks caught his attention for a moment, so Chase turned to flip them over, then he looked back at Megan. "Okay, we'll talk about that first."

She opened her eyes wide, and once again he was

struck by how exceptionally green they looked today. "First? You have a lot on your mind, do you?"

"Yeah, you could say that." Knowing he needed to handle this conversation carefully so he didn't hurt her feelings, he squatted next to her chair, putting him at eye level with her. "I'm not really the carnival type."

"I wasn't expecting you to perform tricks with barn-yard animals."

Ignoring the radiant smile she gave him, he tried again. "No, what I mean is I'm not the type to help on a committee. Just like I'm not the type for a lot of things."

He said the last sentence with meaning in his voice so she would know what he was talking about.

Megan laughed and placed her hand on his forehead. "Are you feeling all right? You're not sick, are you?"

He brushed her hand away and stood, partially because he was annoyed she hadn't caught on to his message, and well, partially because he'd really liked the sensation of her touching him—or rather, he liked it too much.

"I'm fine."

She came over to stand next to him. "Are you sure? Maybe you breathed in too much of Janet's perfume last night and you're having an allergic reaction. I read in a new book the library got last week, *Why Life Stinks*, that many people are allergic to certain scents. And just like some scents can make you feel warm or loved or sexy, others can make you violently ill. Maybe Janet's perfume did that to you."

Chase patiently waited for her to finish, then he

said, "I'm not allergic to Janet's perfume, and I feel fine. I want to talk about last night."

Megan settled back in her chair. "Okay. What's up?"

This was more like it. "First I'd rather not co-chair the committee. I'm too busy right now."

"You don't think the playground is a good idea?"

"Well, sure. It's a great idea."

She nodded slowly. "Just not one you're willing to help make happen."

"It's not that I don't wish you every success. And you know I'll help. In some smaller way."

"Then maybe I shouldn't try to do this, either. I'm really busy at the library right now, too. You may have a good point."

Ah, hell. At times like this, he couldn't help wondering if his parents had dropped him on his head as a baby. He didn't seem to be thinking clearly today.

Determined to find a way out of the hole he'd dug for himself, he said carefully, "Of course you should do it. You've told me lots of times how much building that playground means to you. It's one of your dreams. Ever since you were a kid, you always said if you had enough money, you'd build this great playground for everyone to enjoy. Well, now you've got a way to make that happen," he encouraged.

Megan's expression was thoughtful. "So I should make my dream come true, but without the help of my best friend, is that right?"

Dang it all. He hadn't seen that one coming. This hole he'd dug for himself kept getting bigger and bigger. Megan knew he firmly believed that friends helped each other make their dreams come true. She'd neatly nailed him with his own code of ethics. But why did it have to be a carnival?

Scrubbing one hand over his face, he looked at Megan. "Let's talk about something else for a minute."

She smiled at him again. "Okay."

Since he couldn't think of an easy way to say this, he just said it. "All that picturing each other naked stuff got out of hand last night."

Megan kept smiling. "Really? In what way?"

"You and I are friends, Megan. We've been friends most of our lives. We shouldn't go around picturing each other naked." There. He couldn't be much clearer than that.

"I see. But you said it was okay for me to picture you naked if I got nervous," she pointed out.

"I was kidding."

"I see. So instead, we should picture other people naked, not each other. For instance, you can picture Janet naked if you want to, right?"

Chase ran a hand through his hair. "Uh, well, I don't know about that because—"

"And since I'm not close friends with either Nathan or Trent, I can picture one of them naked if I get nervous, right?"

She looked very pleased with herself, and Chase frowned. "You know that isn't what I meant."

"I guess then I'm not exactly sure what you do mean, Chase. I don't see what's wrong with picturing your brothers naked. I'm sure if I concentrated, I could imagine—"

Chase placed one hand over her mouth. He didn't know when aliens had swooped down and stolen the real Megan, but he knew it had happened. The Megan he knew and had known for years didn't act this way.

Her soft lips pressed against the palm of his hand, and even though she didn't move a muscle, Chase felt as if a bolt of lightning shot straight through his body. He dropped his hand and moved quickly away from her as if he'd caught on fire.

"What is with you?" he demanded, annoyed at what was happening with her, and even more annoyed at what was happening with him. When he'd felt her lips against his skin, desire had surged through his body, making his heart pound heavy in his chest.

He did not want to want Megan. No, make that he refused to want Megan. They were friends, and friends didn't lust after each other.

Megan moved closer to him. "Nothing is with me, Chase. But if it makes you feel any better, I promise I'll no longer picture you naked. And since it bothers you so much, I won't picture your brothers naked, either. If I feel the uncontrollable desire to picture anyone naked, I'll picture some other man. Does that make you feel better?"

Of course it didn't make him feel better. "Megan, don't go around picturing anyone naked." Narrowing his eyes, he added, "You're spending way too much time with Leigh. She's a bad influence on you."

Megan laughed, then turned and walked back toward the house. "You're losing it, cowboy."

Yeah, well, tell him something he didn't know. "Megan, we're not through yet," he told her as she reached out to open the door.

Megan turned and looked at him. For several

seconds, she didn't say a word, merely studied him. Then she gave him a tiny smile that was one of the most seductive things Chase had ever seen in his life.

"Oh, I know we're not through yet. Not by a long shot. In fact, we've just begun."

3

"You rock," Leigh said to Megan in the kitchen. "I think Chase is wrapped up tighter than a Christmas present right now."

No kidding, but so was she. Her conversation with Chase left her rattled and flushed. "You could hear us?"

"No. Not all of it, anyway. But I did catch the part about picturing people naked." She frowned.

Oh, no. Megan drew several deep, soothing breaths into her lungs, willing herself to calm down.

"By the way, I agree with Chase. I don't think you should go around picturing Nathan and Trent naked. That seems kind of gross considering how you feel about Chase."

Megan frowned back at Leigh. "I'm not going to picture anyone naked. For the record, though, you started all this with your comment last night."

"Hey, it worked." Leigh opened the refrigerator and pulled out a pitcher of iced tea. "You didn't seem a bit nervous last night."

"Well, I was, and I wouldn't have been if you hadn't made that crack about Chase."

A slow, calculating smile crossed Leigh's face. "Really cinched your girdle, did it, thinking about Chase that way? It's about time you took some action. Chase is too thickheaded to see what's smack in front of his face, but you're a smart lady. I thought you'd never come to your senses."

Megan shook her head slowly. "I'm not even sure myself how to handle this with Chase. You need to let the two of us work things through on our own."

Leigh leaned against the kitchen island and seemed to consider what Megan had said. After a moment, though, she shook her head. "Nah. No can do. If I leave this completely up to you two, you'll probably mess it up."

Megan realized Chase's sister was serious. She really did intend to keep on meddling. But this plan to make Chase change his mind about her was difficult enough without having Leigh doing crazy things. Something could go very wrong if Leigh got involved. Historically, things did go wrong when Leigh got involved.

"You may scare him off," Megan warned. "Chase and I need to settle this ourselves."

Once again, Leigh tipped her head as if considering what Megan had said. After a couple of seconds, she told Megan, "I'll make you a deal. Since this seems so important to you, I'll back off."

Megan smiled, but before she could relax, Leigh held up one hand.

"But if I see you're making a real mess of things, or if I see Chase acting like an idiot about the situation, then all promises are off," Leigh pronounced. "I'm going to jump back into the fray."

Megan glanced around. Once she was certain no one could hear them, she said, "Leigh, that's not fair. This is none of your business."

"Of course, it is. He's my brother. You're my friend. I have a duty to help." Leigh's tone was nothing short of self-righteous. "I would be a terrible person if I didn't make certain that everything worked out."

Megan sighed. This wasn't at all how she wanted to handle this situation. She preferred to outline carefully any plan she had, and if possible, detail it on index cards. Although she knew she couldn't script what she wanted to happen with Chase, she also wasn't happy leaving it up to Leigh's dubious devices.

"I don't want your help," she told Leigh. "It's sweet of you to offer, but this is something I need to do myself."

"I know you do, Meggie." Leigh blew out a loud breath, which ruffled the row of bangs across her forehead. "Oh, okay. I'll try to butt out; I really will. It's just that I'm so excited about the thought of Chase finally getting a life. He'll become an old fuddy-duddy if he doesn't break out of his habits soon. He needs a wife and a family."

Something about the way Leigh delivered this speech made Megan suspicious. The younger woman had obviously given this topic a great deal of thought.

"So, you're doing this out of love for your brother?" Megan asked. "No other reason?"

Leigh grinned. "Oh, yeah. Love for my brother. You

two will be perfect together. I know it. You know it. All we have to do is get him to know it."

Suspicion crept over Megan like a spider. "That's the only reason? Be honest, what's in it for you if this works?"

Leigh blinked, her expression one of complete innocence. "Why, nothing. Nothing is in this for me except happiness for two people I love."

As if Megan believed that. She hadn't been born yesterday. "Let's try this again. What's in it for you?"

Leigh made a big production out of re-tossing an already tossed salad. "For me? I told you; nothing's in it for me except knowing I helped two fellow human beings find love."

"Bunk." Megan turned the question over in her mind, then suddenly saw the light. "You want Chase to butt out of your life, so that's why you're butting into his, right? You think if he gets involved with me, he'll leave you alone."

"Okay, well, maybe. I mean, every blasted time I'm home from college, he's always spoiling my fun. I figure if he's busy having a little fun of his own, then maybe I can finally be left alone. I'm moving back here this summer, and next fall I start student teaching at the high school. I'll have no fun in my life at all if Chase has anything to say about it."

Megan knew by no fun in her life, Leigh actually meant no guys. "But even if Chase does get distracted, you'll still have Nathan and Trent to deal with."

"Yeah, I know." Leigh circled the kitchen island to come stand by Megan. "But don't you honestly think you're meant to be with Chase? Don't you think the two of you could be truly happy?"

Megan felt a sense of happiness just at the thought of spending her life with Chase. It would be perfect. She just knew it. "Yes, I honestly believe we could be very happy. That's why I've decided to try to get him to think of me in a whole new light."

Leigh smiled. "I think so, too. You're the only woman he's let be part of his life for more than a few months. The two of you have been friends forever. He trusts you, and he doesn't trust many people. If anyone can show him love really does exist, it's you. That's why I'm meddling. And that's why I'll keep meddling if you royally mess up."

Megan couldn't help smiling at Leigh's last comment. "Thanks for the vote of confidence."

"Some things are too important to be left to chance."

☙❧

CHASE TOSSED THE BASKETBALL TO NATHAN. "THROW it in."

Nathan caught the ball with an exaggerated "oomph." Then he shot a grin at Trent. "Looks to me like someone's in a bad mood."

Trent laughed. "Yeah, I wonder why."

Chase glared at his younger brothers. "You know, for a couple of deadbeats who just ate my food in my house, you're real comedians. Now play."

Nathan started dribbling the basketball down their makeshift court in back of the garage. Chase tried to stay focused on the game, but it wasn't easy. Dinner tonight had been a disaster. The conversation had been stilted, that is when someone wasn't snickering for no apparent reason. Through it all, Megan had acted like nothing was happening, Sandi with an *i* had gone on and on about shoes, and Leigh had looked like the proverbial cat who had swallowed a canary.

Chase's nerves were raw, and he wanted to let off some steam. As soon as Megan had driven off, he'd dragged his brothers outside to play basketball. Out here at least, he could stop thinking about women in general, and Megan in particular.

When Nathan got even with Chase, he veered off to the right before Chase could steal the ball away.

"Sandi seems nice," Nathan said to Trent.

Trent lunged for the ball, snagging it away from Nathan with no trouble. "Yeah. She's great." He headed in and easily made a basket. After a short and stupid victory dance, he tossed the ball to Chase. "Plus, she can tie a cherry stem into a knot using only her tongue."

Nathan and Chase froze and stared at him.

When he finally recovered, Chase headed toward the basket. "I can see this is another of your deep, meaningful relationships."

Trent chuckled. "Hey, what's wrong with having a little fun?"

"Sooner or later, you have to grow up and be responsible." Nathan recovered the ball after Chase made a basket.

"I'm the chief of police of this town. If that's not responsible, I don't know what is," Trent said.

"You're responsible in your work, but not in your

personal life," Chase felt obligated to point out. "Sandi, just like the rest of your girlfriends, thinks you may get serious about her."

Trent grabbed the ball away from Nathan and stopped the game. "Okay, if we're going to critique each other's lives, why don't we start with you, Chase, since you're the oldest?"

Chase shook his head. The last thing he needed or wanted right now was to get into this kind of discussion with his brothers. All he wanted to do was blow off some tension.

"Forget it. I shouldn't have said anything."

"No way," Trent said. "We're not going to forget it because that's what this is all about. You're freaking out because Megan might actually have feelings for you, and you're making us pay for it." He grinned at Nathan. "I just love this, don't you?"

Nathan nodded. "Yeah, it is fun."

Chase ignored their teasing. "So you noticed it, too? She's acting strangely."

"No, she's not. She's acting like a woman who is interested in you." Nathan slapped Chase on the back. "Face it, big brother, she wants you bad."

Chase groaned as his brothers dissolved into laughter. Great. Just great. When they finally caught their breath, he said, "Not to spoil your fun, but did it ever occur to you that Megan's going to get hurt if she doesn't cut this out? Love doesn't last, and she's kidding herself if she thinks we can ever have anything together."

"What if you're the one who's wrong?" Nathan asked.

"I'm not, and I bet she's acting this way because she'll be thirty soon." Chase nodded to himself, turning the idea over in his mind. "She probably decided since I'm the only guy in her life at the moment, she'd see if she could make something happen. If I leave things alone for a while, everything will go back to normal."

Trent and Nathan looked at each other, then dissolved into laughter once again.

"What is with you clowns? I'm asking your opinion on how to handle this so I don't end up hurting Megan and destroying our friendship. You could help a little. Jeez." He grabbed the ball away from Nathan and shot another basket.

After a few seconds, his brothers trotted over to stand next to him.

"Okay, you want help. We'll help," Trent said. "The way I see it, you're probably right. Megan is feeling restless, and you're around. If you want to discourage her from having romantic thoughts about you, go on the defensive."

Chase opened his mouth to argue, but then realized his brother had a good point. "I'm listening."

"You need to come on to her," Nathan said. "When she flirts with you, flirt back. Or better yet, you flirt first. Knowing Megan, she'll come to her senses, realize what a mistake this is, and go back to being your friend."

Chase considered the idea for a second, then worry set in. "But what if she takes my flirting seriously? That will make things worse. She'll start thinking we're going to live happily ever after."

Trent shook his head. "Naw, she won't. Because

worst case, you kiss her a couple of times, show her
there's no sexual chemistry between the two of you, and
wham! She'll be out looking for a different guy. Someone
who can—"

"Tie cherry stems with his tongue," Nathan
supplied.

He and Trent both laughed once again.

Chase frowned. "Stop it." For several long moments,
he stared at his brothers, debating whether they were
right. He'd already tried the direct approach with
Megan. Or at least, he'd tried to try the direct approach
with her. Maybe this was the best way to solve the problem. A little harmless flirtation. A kiss or two. She'd
quickly see there was nothing sexual between them.

A picture of her naked slammed into his mind.

Okay, maybe this wasn't such a good idea after all.
Maybe he should simply avoid her. For a few days. Or
weeks. Or surely a couple of years would solve this
problem.

"I don't know," he admitted. "I don't want Megan to
end up getting hurt."

"Which is why you're such a nice guy," Nathan
said. "But trust us, this is the kindest way to handle
the situation. It lets Megan make the final decision.
And what can go wrong? It's not like the two of you
would burn up the sheets if you ever did have sex,
right? I mean, if you were overcome with animal lust
for her, you would have done something about it
before now."

Chase wasn't a hundred percent sure about that.
He'd noticed before that Megan was attractive. Beautiful, even, especially when she was excited about some-

thing. Her face lit up; her eyes seemed to sparkle, and her body came alive.

More than a few times over the years, he'd found himself thinking about Megan in a definitely un-friend-like manner. For instance, every time she came over to swim at the ranch. The woman was hot in a swimsuit, even if she did favor one-pieces that didn't show much. And he'd noticed her body whenever she stopped by to go riding and had on her favorite pair of old jeans that hugged her like a lover's hands.

The dull throbbing in the back of Chase's head returned. When he realized his brothers stood waiting for him to say something, the best he could manage was, "I guess."

"No guessing about it," Trent said. "If you two were wild for each other, you would have seduced her years ago in your pickup like you did half a dozen other girls."

The dull throbbing in his head became a stabbing pain. Being with Megan like that, in a hot-and-heavy session in his old truck, had never seemed right. And in the years since, when his lovemaking had moved from inside cars to inside his house, he'd never felt that he and Megan were meant to be lovers.

They were friends, and true friends were hard to find.

"Maybe. But I also never thought of her that way because Megan wants to get married and have children. Things I don't want. This playground idea of hers is because someday she wants her own children to be able to play in the park."

"Listen, Chase, don't worry about this so much," Nathan advised. "Try things our way. Help Megan with

the carnival. Be a good friend to her. And if she keeps
flirting with you, flirt a little back. Like we said, kiss her
a couple of times. Everything will work out. You'll see."

Except Chase wasn't nearly as certain as Nathan and
Trent seemed to be. "And what if we're all wrong? What
if she takes me seriously and I end up breaking her
heart? What happens then?"

His brothers were silent for several long seconds,
then finally Nathan offered an answer. "If that happens,
you'd need to be a good friend to her and help her put
her heart back together. But at least you'd have let her
find out for herself that you and love don't mix. I don't
see any other way to handle the situation."

"Me, neither," Trent agreed. "You gotta let the lady
figure out for herself that you're the wrong guy for her."
He yanked the basketball out of Chase's arms.

"It really will work out," Nathan said.

Chase still wasn't sure. The only problem was, he
didn't have a better plan than the one his brothers
proposed. "I hope so."

They went back to playing basketball, with Chase
winning by a wide margin. Had to be all his pent-up
stress because he rarely beat his brothers.

As they headed back inside the house, Trent
grinned. "Oh, yeah, since you're so old, you've probably
forgotten how this works; remember that if you and
Megan do decide to take up playing indoor sports, play
safe."

Chase hung his head. The water. There was definitely something screwy with the water in this town.

🦋 4 🦋

Megan glanced around her crowded living room. As far as she could tell, almost every single or divorced woman in town had volunteered to help on the playground committee now that Chase was the co-chair.

All she could figure was that since Chase was always busy with his ranch, these ladies had decided if they wanted to get his attention, they needed to grab this opportunity.

Talk about filling your team with competition. But Megan refused to worry about it. If Chase decided he was interested in one of the other women, she'd simply have to accept it. Might take a while, but she'd accept it. At least then she'd know where she stood with him, and at least she would've tried to make this work.

"Rather than waiting any longer, let's get started," Megan said.

"But, honey, Chase isn't here yet," Janet said

smoothly. "It would be inappropriate not to wait for him."

Speaking of inappropriate, that halter top Janet had on was more than a little indecent. Megan opened her mouth to point this out when it occurred to her she was being catty, so she slammed her mouth shut. She would not turn into a name-calling shrew simply because she'd decided to show Chase how she felt about him.

"I think Megan is right," Amanda Newman said. As the wife of the minister and the only married woman in the room, Megan decided to sit next to her. If things got out of hand, Amanda could be the voice of reason.

"Oh, all right." Janet flounced over to the couch and sat. Immediately, two of her best friends from high school, Tammy Holbrook and Sally Estes, sat on either side of her. Eventually, the rest of the women found seats as well.

Megan began the meeting by recapping what she'd said to the city council. As she spoke, she quickly realized that only Amanda was paying the slightest bit of attention to her. Everyone else was listening for Chase to arrive.

Just great.

Amanda tugged gently on the sleeve of Megan's red dress. Megan leaned toward her, and the older woman said, "I think now would be a good time to make the assignments."

Baffled, Megan leaned back. Make the assignments? But no one was paying attention to her. If she made the assignments now...oh, yeah. Megan smiled. Excellent idea.

"So, Janet, you and Tammy will head up refreshments, right? You'll need to arrange for plenty of sodas and food."

From across the room, Janet nodded vaguely, her gaze still on Megan's front door. "Sure, whatever. Just put my name down."

Megan bit back a smile. This was going to be much easier than she'd expected. In fact, during the next ten minutes, she made almost all of the assignments, and no one raised a finger to stop her.

She'd just finished filling in Sally's name for the job of finding prizes to give out to the winners of the carnival games when the sound of a pickup pulling up silenced the group.

"Showtime," Amanda murmured with a smile.

Megan didn't have the chance to let Chase into the house because before she could even stand, three women were by the door, welcoming him. Chase looked startled when he walked in, but within a couple of seconds, he looked practically horrified.

"Am I the only man here?" he growled to Megan when he finally made it across the room.

"I'm afraid so. But don't worry. We have plenty of volunteers," she said.

And every one of those volunteers—with the exception of Amanda—was looking at Chase as if he were a half-price silk blouse at a one-day-only sale. Megan knew even she was staring at him.

But who could blame them? Freshly showered and shaved, smelling like a clean healthy male and looking like a movie star, Chase Barrett was enough to get any female heart racing.

Not surprisingly, he was offered almost any and

every chair in the room. Janet even offered to let him have her seat, and of course, she'd be happy to sit in his lap. But Chase just said thanks and sat on the ottoman by Megan's chair. A silly schoolgirl thrill ran through her when he chose to be near her, and Megan mentally berated herself on being so petty. This wasn't a game she was playing. Unlike most of the women in the room, she wasn't interested in having wild, crazy sex with Chase simply so she could brag to her friends.

She was interested in love, commitment, and family. She glanced at him briefly, but when his dark-blue gaze met her own, her pulse fluttered, her breathing grew shallow, and she forced herself to look away.

Okay, she wouldn't mind a little of that wild sex being thrown in as a bonus. But that wasn't her main goal. Her main goal was to show him she could make him happy. Truly happy. For life. Not just during one afternoon of frantic, yeehaw, ride 'em cowboy sex.

Chase waved one hand in front of her face, and Megan jumped.

"You okay in there, Megan?" Chase teased. "You have a funny look on your face."

Oh, she'd just bet she did. "I'm fine," she said, cringing when her voice came out way too breathless and far too squeaky.

"So how's it going?" he asked.

Immediately, several of the women launched into a description to bring Chase up-to-date. Almost all of them were surprised to learn that at some point, they'd volunteered to head up a particular task. But thankfully, they all took their job assignments in good stride. Even

Janet said it wouldn't be the first time she couldn't remember what she'd promised to do.

"I promised my first husband I'd love him forever, and look how that turned out," she said with a laugh.

"Love needs care to make it flourish," Amanda said.

Pretty much everyone's expression made it clear they disagreed with Amanda, but since she was the minister's wife and a really nice lady in her own right, no one made a comment. Personally, Megan thought Amanda was right. Love did need care and attention. But now was not the time, and this was not the crowd, to open the question up for debate.

"Anyway, we're now down to finding items for the auction," Megan said. "Earl has volunteered to let us use his big party tent to have the auction in. Nathan's donating a laptop. But we need a lot of other items as well so we can make enough money."

"I talked to my sister last night, and she's willing to help," Amanda said. "She owns a bed and breakfast in San Antonio and is willing to donate a room for two for a weekend."

Megan smiled. "That's wonderful."

"If you're married," Janet said with a snort. "What if one of us single women wants to bid? What about tossing in someone to escort us on this trip if we win?" She scanned the room as if considering what to say next, but Megan knew without a doubt that Janet had this all planned out. "What about if the winning bidder so chooses, then Chase will be her escort for the weekend?"

Megan expected Amanda to protest, but instead,

she seemed delighted by the idea. "I'm sure my sister will donate an extra room if that happens."

"Whoa, whoa. Hold on here a minute," Chase said. "I'm not going to be a gigolo prize in the auction."

"Of course not, dear," Amanda said. "The prize is the free hotel room near the River Walk in San Antonio. You'd only be the escort if the winner decides she wants one. And then naturally, you'd request the separate room, but this way, the lady could enjoy the trip in the company of a man she could trust."

It all sounded so tame and reasonable coming from Amanda, but the hot looks several of the women were directing at Chase made it clear the last thing they would want on the trip was a man they could trust.

"I still don't like it," Chase muttered. "But okay, just so long as everyone's clear about this up front. I'm not a stud service." He glanced at Amanda. "Pardon my language."

She smiled. "No problem."

Megan bit back her own smile and made a mental note to check the latest balance on her savings account. There was no way she was going to let Janet Defries win that prize. If anyone was going away for a romantic weekend with Chase, it was going to be her.

CHASE WAS HALFWAY HOME WHEN HE PULLED OFF TO the side of the road, hooked a U-turn, and headed back to Megan's house. This carnival-auction thing was getting out of hand. Now he was one of the prizes. And no way would he believe for a second that one of the single women in town wasn't going to win. He'd seen the way they'd looked at him. When one woman looked at you that way, it was nice. When ten looked at you with hunger in their eyes, it was downright scary.

Everyone was gone by the time he pulled back into Megan's driveway. No doubt they'd scattered as soon as he'd left. After slamming his truck into Park, he sprinted to her front door and rapped loudly. A couple of seconds later, the light in the living room came on, and Megan opened the door.

"Don't you ask who it is before you fling open your front door in the middle of the night..." His gaze dropped and scanned her body. "Wearing hardly any clothes," he barely managed to say.

Because she was wearing hardly any clothes, or at least, she looked that way. She had on a short pink nightie that clung to her every curve. Backlit as she was from the light inside the house, Chase now knew he wouldn't have to guess the next time he wanted to picture Megan naked.

"Oops." She dashed toward the back of the house.

Chase came inside and shut the door behind him. He could only hope Megan was putting on a long, thick terry cloth robe. But when she came back out from her bedroom, she actually had on a flowered, silky robe that came to the top of her knees. It wasn't a whole lot better than the nightie, but it was at least something.

"Why are you here?" she asked.

He'd been staring at her robe, his blood pounding hot and heavy through his body as he remembered what she'd looked like seconds ago, but at her question, he yanked his gaze back to her face. What had she asked? Oh, yeah, why was he here.

"I'm not having sex with those women so you can build a playground in the park," he told her.

Rather than being upset, Megan laughed and curled up on the couch. "No one is asking you to do that, Chase."

"Janet wants me to. And so do those other women." He flopped down next to her on the couch, making certain he left plenty of room between them.

"All you have to say is no, and if you really don't want to go, I'll talk to Amanda, and we'll change the prize."

This was more like it. This was the sane, responsible Megan he knew. "Well, okay then."

She laughed again, and the soft sound floated around him. "You know, the easy solution is to have me place the winning bid on the weekend package," Megan said. "That way, you won't have to feel like a gigolo."

Her suggestion sounded reasonable enough, but it sure didn't feel that way to him. Going away to a bed and breakfast on the River Walk with Megan while all this flirting stuff was going on between them didn't feel reasonable at all.

It sounded hot—and dangerous.

"I'm not sure that would be a good idea," he said.

"Are you afraid I'll seduce you?"

"No." That wasn't the problem at all. At the moment, thinking about her in that nightie, he was afraid he'd try to seduce her. But the carnival was weeks away. Maybe by that time, Megan would come to her senses about them, and their friendship could return to normal.

She sat tucked in the corner of the couch, watching him. Waiting for him to say more.

He scrubbed his face with his hands, feeling as cornered as a calf in a roping competition. "Okay, fine. If your committee insists on auctioning this weekend trip, then you'd better be the one to win it. I'll give you money so you—"

"I have money saved. I can pay for it myself." The day he did that was the day he'd hang up his saddle and build himself a pine box. "No way are you paying, Megan. I am. I'll buy this trip to San Antonio."

"But don't you think Janet and the other women will be annoyed when they find out you bought the trip yourself?"

Boy, this was more complicated than figuring out a mutt's parentage. "Fine. I'll give you the money, and you buy the trip. Just make certain you don't lose."

Her smile was downright blissful. "Sounds like a great idea, and I promise, I won't lose."

"But we're going to have separate rooms. We're going as friends, because that's what we are and have always been. Say it with me...friends."

"Friends." She said the word slowly, but with a sexual overtone that made his heart race fast and furious.

Chase blew out an aggravated breath. He wanted whatever was going on here to stop. He wanted his life to get back to normal.

He wanted the old Megan back. He didn't want to picture her naked, didn't want to think about either of them seducing the other, didn't want to lose her friendship.

But he also was having no luck getting the image of her in that nightie out of his head.

"I want to talk to you about what's been going on," he finally said. "This whole thing with you and me. It can't work."

Her expression was innocent, but he could see the pulse beating wildly in her neck. She was far from calm.

"What thing would that be?" she asked.

Okay, so that was the way she planned on playing this. Fine.

"You've been flirting with me."

She blinked. "I have?"

"You know you have. You've never flirted with me before."

She nibbled on her bottom lip, and Chase barely bit back a groan. Did she know she was turning him on? Did she really mean to drive him wild?

Apparently, since she continued nibbling on her bottom lip for a good ten seconds. Finally, he couldn't stand it anymore.

"Megan, do you want to have sex with me? Is that what this is about? You're lonely. I'm convenient."

Even in the muted light of the cozy living room, he could clearly see the blush that climbed her face. But she never looked away from him. She kept her gaze locked on his face.

"What would you do if I said yes?"

Chase felt like someone sucker-punched him in the gut. The breath in his lungs seemed to whoosh out of his body.

"You seriously want to have sex with me?" he finally managed to ask when he remembered how to talk. He hadn't expected her to be so blunt.

"Among other things." Her voice was even softer than before, and he had to strain to hear her clearly. "But not because I'm lonely. And not because you're convenient."

"I see." But he didn't at all. He didn't understand any of this. "Mind if I ask why now? Why after all these years? Is it because of your clock?"

"Clock?"

He waved one hand. "You know. Your biological clock. Is this about having babies?"

She smiled at his comment. "No, my biological clock has nothing to do with this."

"Then what does? What's got you acting this way?"

She remained silent for so long that he wondered for a second if she intended on answering him. Finally, she said, "Maybe I'm tired of not going after what I want in life." She drew in a deep breath, then added, "Going after the man I want in my life."

All sorts of emotions roared through Chase. For starters, he was flattered that he meant so much to her. Then he was annoyed that she was ruining the only successful relationship he'd ever had with a woman. And finally, he was undeniably turned on.

But one conclusion was unavoidable. He needed to talk her out of this.

"We're good friends, Megan. Sex would ruin everything. Getting involved on any personal level would destroy the friendship we've had for twenty years."

"How do you know that? What if it makes everything better?"

How could she be so naive? She knew about his past, how his dad had bailed on the family one winter morning simply because he'd decided he was in love with a waitress from the local diner. She also knew about each one of his failed relationships, just as he knew about hers. They'd both tried several times to make love last, and it had disappeared quicker than a sinner on Sunday morning.

Those times, when what they thought was love turned out to be hormones, they'd moved on. Wiser. A little sadder. But not brokenhearted.

But this time, when the relationship ended, he'd lose his best friend. The woman he'd grown up with. The one true friend who had shared his life.

The price was just too high.

"It won't make everything better," he muttered. "You and I both know it won't. And then what will happen? Will we still be friends?"

"Of course."

"I can't help thinking you'll end up hating me."

He shifted closer to her on the couch. "I've tried, but love doesn't last. It didn't last for my parents. It doesn't last for me. You've had relationships, too. They didn't last."

Her green eyes sparkled with conviction when she said, "It could be different for us. We could be one of the lucky couples. One of the couples who finds true and lasting love."

Her soft voice enticed him to believe, but he

couldn't let her fool herself this way. She deserved better. "It won't work, Megan."

"Because you're a heartbreaker."

Turning his head, he studied her. "Maybe. That's what the ladies in this town tell me."

She leaned toward him, the motion making the top of the robe open a tiny bit. Although Chase knew she didn't mean the action to be seductive, it was. He could now see just a sliver of her pink nightie. He stared at that small patch of cloth for a moment, trying not to think about the soft skin underneath. When his gaze finally met hers again, he felt the look clear to his soul.

"You don't always have to be a heartbreaker. You don't have to break my heart," she said.

Chase shut his eyes and leaned back against the couch. Megan was set on this, and it looked as if she was going to remain set on this until he proved her wrong.

Trent and Nathan's suggestion surfaced in his mind. Was that really the way to handle this situation? Should he prove her wrong, show her that the chemistry they shared would fade, as it always faded?

He tipped his head and looked at her. "Kiss me."

She blinked several times in rapid succession. "What?"

Okay, this was more like it. He'd thrown her. About time.

"I asked you to kiss me. You're telling me you want us to have sex. Well, I figure we should start out with a kiss. Who knows, maybe the kiss will rank up there with catching the flu. Maybe after that, you'll find out you aren't so hot for me after all."

She laughed, her eyes dancing with humor. "Oh, I see. This is a test. You don't think I'll really kiss you."

"Oh, no, I believe you will. I'm just not sure you'll like it. We're friends, Megan. We probably have zip in the way of sexual chemistry. But hey, it you want to give it a try, then it's fine by me. Kiss me."

She narrowed her eyes. "I can't simply kiss you."

"Why not?"

She waved one hand as if searching for the words. "Because you lead up to a kiss. You share a romantic evening. You talk about your feelings. You don't just grab someone and kiss them."

"Why not?" he asked again.

"It's not romantic."

He shrugged. "I'm not a romantic guy. You know that."

Her expression softened. "Yes, you are. You're very romantic."

His heart seemed to lurch in his chest, but he refused to let her see this was getting to him. But it was. He was more than ready to show her anything she wanted.

But that was his hormones kicking in. It was late. She was practically naked and staring at him with desire in her eyes. He was a red-blooded, healthy male.

Of course his engine was racing.

But if Megan insisted on playing this game, then she had to be the one to lead it.

"If I'm such a romantic guy, then kiss me," he said.

He expected her to back down, but his request had the opposite effect. She gave him a look that let him know in no uncertain terms that she was on to his trick and wasn't about to fall for it. She slowly scooted forward until she was next to him on the couch. Holding his gaze, she leaned forward and lightly brushed her lips across his.

Chase was totally unprepared for the sensation. It felt like electricity skittered through his body at her touch. For a split second, they both froze. Then she pulled away from him.

"There. I kissed you," she said softly, her face mere inches from his own.

"Ah, now, Megan. That wasn't a kiss." He lightly touched her hair. "Old ladies kiss better than that. Guess I was right. We have no sexual chemistry," he lied.

Her eyes darkened, and she smiled at his obvious fib. "You think you're so smart, don't you?"

He couldn't prevent the grin that crossed his face. "Just pointing out the obvious."

She shoved his shoulder good-naturedly. "You figure you've got this all worked out. I know you. You think I'll chicken out and not give this kissing thing another try."

He chuckled, enjoying having Megan this close to him, even though he knew he shouldn't. "You? Chicken out? Couldn't happen."

She leaned even closer to him, the sweet scent of her citrus shampoo filling his lungs. "Well, if you don't expect me to chicken out, then that means you figure if I give you a real kiss, fireworks won't go off. After that I'll give up and forget the whole thing."

The lady knew him well, but he wasn't going to admit it. "Maybe."

LORI WILDE & LIZ ALVIN

"Maybe my foot." For a second, she assessed him. Then, her expression turned smug. "Okay, cowboy, hold on to your hat."

Chase figured he was prepared for anything she could dish out, but he hadn't counted on Megan half crawling into his lap, cupping his face in her small hands, and kissing him hard.

She almost knocked him off balance with the impact, and out of necessity, he placed his hands on her waist to keep them from toppling over. But if Megan noticed their position, she made no comment. She was too busy kissing him.

And kissing him.

And kissing him.

It took every bit of his resolve to keep from kissing her back. He hadn't expected his body to respond to her the way it was, as if he'd been dying of thirst for a very long time and she was giving him sustenance.

But he knew she was wrong about this. So what if her kisses were setting his blood on fire? He'd been alone for some time, and Megan was soft and sweet.

"Kiss me back, Chase," she murmured against his lips. "Just this once. Kiss me back."

He shifted his head, so his lips pressed against her cheek. "I don't think so."

Megan squirmed against him until he groaned and stopped her. Through the thinness of her robe, he could feel how soft and warm her body was. His experiment ranked right up there with Dr. Frankenstein's. He'd created a monster, and he had no idea how much longer he could hold out.

"Give me one real kiss, Chase," Megan whispered

again. "If it doesn't drive us both wild, then I'll stop flirting with you. I promise."

At this point, Chase figured the sooner they got this experiment over with, the better. Finally, even though he knew he was making one humongous mistake, he relented.

"Fine," he said. "One kiss."

Megan rewarded him with a dimpled smile. "Thank you."

This time when she leaned forward and kissed him, he buried his hands in her hair, damned his own soul, and kissed her back.

❦ 5 ❦

Chase's kiss was every bit as perfect as Megan had known it would be.

Maybe even a little bit more perfect than expected, since his kiss alone was enough to shoot her libido sky-high. She'd never kissed anyone before who made her want to toss him to the ground and take wanton advantage of him.

But she sure wanted to with Chase.

Instead, she settled for this kiss, this one chance to show Chase just how amazing they were together. Without waiting for him to take the initiative, Megan touched the tip of her tongue to his bottom lip. Joy rushed through her when he complied with her silent request by parting his lips. Now they were getting somewhere.

For long, languid minutes, they lost themselves in a kiss that was so much more than the mere meeting of lips. It was fireworks, shooting stars, and magic all rolled into one. Megan was positive that Chase felt the electricity dance between them every bit as much as she did. How could he not? They were meant to be together.

With a loud groan, Chase finally broke the kiss. He opened his eyes and stared at her. He looked totally dazed, with maybe a touch of horrified thrown in, sort of like he'd just been kicked in the head by his favorite horse.

He was stunned.

Good.

Stunned she could work with. Megan smiled, offering him reassurance. She appreciated that their situation was new to Chase. He hadn't had a lot of time to adjust to the idea of being more than just friends. No doubt the incendiary nature of the kiss had been a surprise to him.

"That was something else," she said, caressing the side of his face with the gentlest of touches.

Chase leaned away from her hand. Then he cleared his throat. Twice. And blinked. Twice.

"Are you okay?" she asked.

He jerked his head in what she assumed was a nod. Then he made an incomprehensible response that sounded like "urpuft," and shifted her so she no longer straddled his lap. Once she was off him, he stood so quickly he almost seemed to shoot off the couch. "I gotta go."

Not exactly the reaction she'd hoped for, but certainly understandable.

"Okay." She gave him another encouraging smile.

He ran his hands through his hair and blew out a

loud breath. Then he turned and stared at her, desire still heating his blue gaze. "Megan, about that kiss..."

Her heart rate quickened. She knew he was going to tell her how wonderful, how incredible, how miraculous the kiss had been. Maybe he'd ask her to kiss him again. "Yes?"

He cleared his throat again. "That kiss was what I thought it would be. Don't get me wrong—it was okay. A good kiss between friends. But like I said, there's no chemistry between us, so it didn't exactly rock the world."

Openmouthed, Megan stared at him. What? The man had lost his mind. No chemistry? He knew that wasn't true.

Her gut reaction was to argue with him, to point out as nicely as possible that he was full of hooey. But her instincts warned her that was the wrong approach. She shut her mouth, understanding flowing through her. Chase needed time. She'd pushed him too hard, too fast. No wonder he was denying what was obvious.

She'd read a book last week that talked about this exact situation—*Fit to be Tied*. According to the author, even when a man was ready for a lasting relationship, old habits often died hard. These men lied about their feelings, even to themselves. Sometimes the lies were tiny. Sometimes they weren't.

In Chase's case, he was telling himself a whopper of a lie. A gargantuan lie. As his friend, it was her duty to help him face the truth. To do that, she needed to give him time to adjust to the inferno they'd generated when they'd kissed. Time for him to accept reality.

The best approach as far as she could tell was to go

along with his cockamamie statement that the kiss had been nothing special. So to help him in the long run, she'd agree.

Unfolding herself from the couch, she stood. "You're right. The kiss wasn't a big deal. At least now we know that kissing each other is like sucking on a dead fish."

Chase frowned, but at least her statement seemed to snap him out of the daze he'd been in. "A dead fish? Hold on there, Megan. I didn't say it wasn't enjoyable. Just that it...you know, we're friends. It was a kiss between friends."

Megan bit back a smile at his defensive tone. Please. Friends only kissed that way if they were about to have wild and crazy sex. Enjoyable was the understatement of the year, but once again, she didn't argue.

"True. It was a simple little kiss between friends. I realize now how silly I was to expect fireworks between us. It was pleasant, but I've certainly had better."

That got him. Megan had never seen anyone manage to frown on top of an already existing frown, but Chase pulled it off. Megan resisted the impulse to tell him that his face might freeze like that. Instead, she focused all her attention on getting him to believe her ridiculous lie. Chase knew as well as she did that neither of them had ever experienced a kiss remotely as fantastic.

He folded his arms across his chest. "The kiss was a mite better than pleasant."

Keeping her tone light and casual, she said, "I guess. A little bit, maybe." When he opened his mouth, presumably to argue with her, Megan hurriedly added, "Well, if you'll excuse me, I need to get my rest. Tomorrow is a busy day."

"You're kicking me out?"

The smile she'd been holding back broke free. She ended up grinning like a schoolgirl. "You need to go home now. Have a nice night."

Without waiting for him to follow her, she led the way to her front door. Opening it, she watched him walk out, her smile only growing as he passed by her muttering about women and the water and the world in general.

"Drive safely," she told Chase, feeling positively delighted with how the evening had turned out. Tonight, Chase had kissed her. Really kissed her. And fireworks had happened, even if he wasn't ready to admit they'd been anything more than sparklers.

She and Chase were perfect together. Just as she'd known they would be.

Things could only get better from here.

🐚

THIS WAS A DISASTER. A FULL-FLEDGED, THE-BARN'S-on fire disaster. Chase sat in his truck, still parked outside Megan's house. He watched her turn off the lights in the living room. She was going to bed, and he hated the fact that he wanted to join her in that bed.

He really, *really* wanted to join her in that bed. But it couldn't—make that wouldn't—happen. He rubbed his forehead as frustration crept up his spine and crouched in his neck muscles.

Man, why had he agreed to that kiss? He was smarter than that. He'd stepped right into that trap like a blind fool. Now his life was even more catawampus than it had been before, and he had no one to blame but himself.

But come on, how was he supposed to know a simple kiss from Megan would shake him right down to his boots? That heat and desire and good-old want would flare to the point that he felt as if he'd literally caught on fire?

And what had she meant with that crack about having had better kisses? That was physically impossible. No one had ever had a better kiss than the one they'd shared.

Maybe it had been a fluke. He'd been Megan's friend for a long, long time. If they truly did have that kind of amazing chemistry between them, he would have felt it before now, right? So the kiss had to be a fluke.

But even knowing the combustible kiss had been a fluke didn't change the simple fact that he needed to be reasonable about this. They had to ignore this aberration in their friendship. His brothers had been wrong. Dead wrong. He needed to squash this attraction he felt toward Megan like a big old spider. No evasion. No hesitation.

He started his truck and backed out of Megan's driveway. When he'd put a couple of miles between them, he felt much better. Now, with the sizzle from the kiss gone, he was positive it had been a fluke. So, with a little effort, he could put it behind him.

By tomorrow, he and Megan would be back to their usual friendship, and this kissing nonsense would be over. They'd once again be pals, hanging around together, sharing jokes, kidding each other.

But no more kissing. From this point on, the two of them were going to keep their lips to themselves.

❧❧

MEGAN GLANCED OVER THE NEW BOOKS SHE NEEDED to catalog. Two romances, a mystery, an assortment of children's books, and three new self-help books. Two of them dealt with child-rearing, something she currently had no use for, but with any luck, would someday soon.

The last book caught her eye—*Browbeating for the Naturally Shy*. Now there was something she could use. Not that she intended on browbeating Chase, but she did need to be more assertive, especially now. No doubt Chase intended on avoiding any more physical contact with her, which of course would make getting him to kiss her again a bit of a challenge. But she needed him to kiss her again so he could see that the fire of the first kiss hadn't been a one-time wonder.

She opened her desk drawer and pulled out a stack of index cards. What she needed was a plan.

"You're handling him all wrong," Leigh said as she breezed into the office.

Megan glanced up. The younger woman stood just inside the doorway with her hands on her hips, a frown on her pretty face. Seems like all Megan did these days was cause members of the Barrett family to frown at her.

"What are you talking about?" Megan asked.

Leigh dropped into the chair facing Megan's desk. "Chase. You're handling him all wrong."

"I'm not handling him at all," she told Leigh.

"Sure, you are. You're trying to trap him—"

"No, I'm not."

Leigh groaned. "Fine. You're trying to lure him—"

Megan was the one to groan this time. "Leigh, I'm not trying to handle, trap, or lure your brother into anything."

Leaning forward, Leigh said, "Call it whatever you want, but you want to make my brother fall in love with you. Right?"

An unsettling feeling lodged in Megan's stomach. She sincerely didn't want to trick Chase into anything. She believed in being forthright and honest at all times. She'd never try something so completely underhanded.

She glanced at the blank index cards sitting in front of her and inwardly cringed. But those cards were for a plan, and a plan was different than a trap, right? Just because she wanted to think of ways to make Chase notice her as a woman didn't mean she was trapping him.

Did it?

She looked at Leigh. "I'm not trying to make your brother fall in love with me. I'm hoping that our friendship and affection for each other can grow naturally into something deeper and more profound."

For a moment, Leigh stared at her. Then she made a snorting noise and said, "Pig slop."

"It is not pig slop. It's how I feel."

"Megan, hon, I love you like a sister, but there're a couple of things wrong with what you said. First up, you got Chase on your committee so you could try to get him to fall for you."

Megan sat up straighter in her chair. "Excuse me,

Leigh, but I didn't get Chase on my committee, you did. You backed him into a corner, so he had no choice but to agree to help."

Leigh waved one hand. "Semantics. You. Me. It doesn't really matter. All that matters is that he was forced onto your committee."

Megan sighed. Leigh was...well, Leigh. The woman could make a tornado seem tame by comparison. And to be completely honest, regardless of who had gotten him on the committee, Megan was thrilled he'd ended up there. Moreover, Leigh was right. She did intend on using the committee as a way to spend more time with him.

But that didn't mean she was luring, trapping, or tricking the man. She was simply giving him lots of opportunities to realize his feelings for her.

Megan frowned. Maybe she wasn't being quite as forthright with Chase as she thought, but she wasn't handling him. Images of last night flashed in her brain. Okay, she'd handled him somewhat last night, but not in the way Leigh meant.

With another sigh, this time directed at herself, Megan looked at her friend. "Why are you here?"

Leigh chuckled. "Got you tangled up, huh?" When Megan didn't respond, she continued, "I'm here because Chase is being a colossal pain today. Whatever you did to him last night has got him stomping around muttering about you."

That didn't sound good. "Muttering about me? Is he angry?"

"Can't tell. I've never seen him like this. He's jumpy and snarly. Chase is the most easygoing guy in the world. Usually I have to hold a mirror in front of his face to make sure he's still alive. But not today. Today he's more jittery than a werewolf in a silver-bullet factory."

Megan turned this information over in her mind. Jumpy, snarly, and jittery didn't sound like Chase. Not at all. Maybe this was a good sign. Maybe the kiss had thrown him for a loop, and he didn't know what to make of it. Maybe this was the first step in Chase coming to terms with his feelings for her. This could be a very good sign.

Then again, maybe it was the first step in him deciding to never see her again. Maybe he was so mad at her that he'd never want to see her again. Uh-oh. This could be a really bad, bad sign. Leigh sat staring at her, obviously expecting her to say something. Unclear what the younger woman wanted to hear, Megan settled for, "Sorry he's grumpy."

"Grumpy? He's a lot more than grumpy. He told me this morning that we have too many toothpicks in the house. Toothpicks, Megan. He's talking about toothpicks."

"And that means?" Megan asked, trying to understand what could possibly have bothered Chase about toothpicks.

Leigh rolled her eyes. "Heck if I know. He's not himself. At first, I thought you'd managed to shake him up, and that he'd finally get a clue about how he feels about you. Now I'm not so sure. Chase can be stubborn. He may ricochet the other way and decide the safest approach is not to have anything to do with you."

Megan felt as if her heart dropped to her shoes.

Surely Leigh wasn't right. "He'll probably calm down soon."

Leigh leaned forward. "Just in case he doesn't, let me give you a hand in getting him to fall for you."

No way. Leigh was a walking, talking trouble magnet. Her interference would only upset the precarious balance Megan had created with Chase. These things needed to be handled delicately, and the word delicate wasn't in Leigh's vocabulary.

"I appreciate your offer, but I want to handle this myself," Megan told her. "I realize I may have confused your brother, but I still believe if he's given enough time, he'll come to see we're meant to be together."

Leigh tipped her head and studied Megan. "You honestly believe that, don't you?"

"I certainly do. I think Chase will respond best if I approach him with honesty and compassion."

Leigh bobbed her head, but Megan suspected she wasn't really listening. The younger woman simply waited until Megan finished speaking, then blurted, "I'll tell you what Chase will respond to. You call him up, tell him you need to talk to him about the fundraiser, then you show up at the ranch wearing racy undies and holding a can of whipped cream. The boy will come around real quick after that." Leigh's smile turned devilish. "If he doesn't keel over from a heart attack, he'll be yours for life."

Megan's mouth dropped open about halfway through Leigh's suggestion and refused to shut no matter how hard she tried. Racy underwear? Whipped cream?

"I could never do something like that," Megan

finally managed to squeak out when Leigh stopped speaking. "I'd feel like a..."

"An assertive, independent woman?" Leigh winked. "It sure would take his mind off the toothpick problem, I can guarantee you that."

For one second, the image Leigh had created slithered through Megan's mind. She could almost see Chase's expression when he opened the door to find her standing there in racy undies. She'd give him her sexiest smile, squirt a dollop of whipped cream on one finger, then slip it into his mouth and...

Oh, my.

Megan took a deep breath, trying to mentally quell her libido and throw a bucket of ice water on the image she'd created in her mind. Whatever else she did over the next few weeks, she most certainly wasn't going to show up on Chase's doorstep barely dressed.

This was about love. Not sex.

Thinking that Megan's silence meant she'd found a convert, Leigh warmed to her subject. "If you don't like whipped cream, there's always strawberry jam. Or chili. Chase likes chili."

Megan's mouth tried to drop open again, but she stopped it. Chili? What in the world would she do with chili? Megan refused to even think about that one.

"I'm not seducing your brother. I'm not showing up at the ranch in racy undies. And I'm not bringing food of any sort with me," Megan maintained firmly. "Chase and I will sort this out on our own without tricks."

Leigh sighed and stood. "I figured you'd be unreasonable. Fine. Do it your way. But just so you know, I'm not going to spend the next few weeks living with a man who complains about how many toothpicks we have in the house. Something's going to give, and it won't be me."

With that as her parting shot, Leigh walked out.

Megan fiddled with the index cards on her desk.

This situation with Chase was confusing enough without having Leigh interfering.

She picked up the book on her desk. Did she really want to browbeat Chase? She knew in her heart that she didn't. She wanted Chase to love her because...well, because he did. She didn't want to trick him into caring.

She pushed the book aside and slipped the index cards back into her desk drawer. She'd rather give up than feel as if she'd deceived Chase.

Besides, as long as he continued to work on the committee with her, she would have plenty of time to get him to notice her as more than a friend.

Plenty of time.

❧ 6 ❧

Chase pulled his truck up in front of the library and turned off the engine. He glanced at the darkened front door and couldn't help wishing he'd missed Megan. He was as nervous as a fifteen-year-old about to ask out a girl for the first time.

"Get a grip, Barrett," he muttered to himself. He threw open the truck door and climbed out. He wasn't going to get weird about one little kiss. Now that he'd had a day to think about it, he was positive the kiss hadn't been a big deal. Sure, it had been a good kiss, maybe even a great kiss, but it was nothing special.

Nothing unusual.

Nothing he couldn't handle.

Determined, he headed toward the library's front door, rapping loudly on the glass. After a couple of seconds, Megan appeared and waved to him. She signaled him to wait, then headed back in the direction of her office.

Chase shifted his weight from one leg to the other.

He wasn't looking forward to this conversation. In fact, if he'd had his way, he would have avoided Megan for a couple of days. Just until things between them settled down.

But Megan had called, saying she needed him to stop by and pick up some papers having to do with the committee.

That was another thing. He sure wished he could think of a way to get off this committee, especially now that he and Megan were so jumpy around each other. But he couldn't do that to her. He was already hurting her by making her face reality when it came to this attraction between them. He couldn't also bail on her committee.

He watched as Megan hurried to the door, twisting the lock.

"Hi," she said, her voice slightly breathless as he walked by her and into the library. He could only hope she was breathless because she'd been scurrying around, not because he was near her.

"Hey." He glanced around the library. They were alone, just as he'd feared.

"Where are Carl and Debbie tonight?" he asked, hoping the other employees of the library were simply hiding somewhere and hadn't left for the day.

"They've already gone home." She gave him a nervous smile, then headed toward her office.

Silently cursing himself, Chase followed. He should have known better than to let her talk him into that kissing nonsense last night. Now Megan was uncomfortable around him. No two ways around it, they needed to forget about all this sexual stuff.

Without intending to, his gaze dropped, and he watched the gentle sway of Megan's hips as she walked. Man, she was one nice-looking lady. Her dark-blue slacks hugged her curves, and he couldn't help wondering what would happen if he—

What in the sweet name of sanity was he doing? He yanked his gaze away and ran his hands through his hair. Twice.

A grip. He needed to get a grip. He once again cursed himself.

Megan turned toward him. "What did you just say?"

He had no idea. He hadn't even realized he'd spoken aloud. "Nothing," he tried, but the look she gave him made it clear she wasn't buying that. She crossed her arms and studied him.

"It sounded suspiciously like you called me a name." The way she was standing drew his attention to her breasts. He remembered all too well what those breasts had looked like last night in that pink nightie she'd had on.

"Yoo-hoo. Chase. Are you all right?"

He pulled his gaze back up to her face, then groaned. What was happening to him? He was losing his mind. Or worse, turning into some sort of degenerate. All he seemed to be doing was staring at parts of Megan that he had no business staring at.

"I wasn't talking to you. I was talking to myself. I called myself a name," he explained, and she had no idea how much he meant it. He was sorry. A sorry son-of-a-horse-trader. "I think maybe we should postpone this meeting."

She took a step toward him. "Aren't you feeling well?"

He debated what to say. He didn't want her to worry that he was sick, but he could hardly tell her what was really bothering him. This was all the fault of that blasted kiss. His gaze landed on her lips. She wasn't wearing lipstick. Her mouth looked soft, and sweet, and oh-so-kissable. He remembered all too well what her lips had felt like pressed against his, her breath mixing with his own.

He blew out a disgusted breath and hung his head. He was dumber than a box of rocks.

"Are you feeling dizzy?" she asked.

He raised his head. "No, I'm not dizzy. And I'm not sick. I'm..." He didn't want to talk about what he was feeling on any level. What was wrong with him could be cured with a long, cold shower.

She had on her glasses, which she now nudged up her small nose. "Are you confused because of what happened last night?"

Grabbing that excuse like a drowning man lunging for a life preserver, he said, "Yeah. That's it. The kiss last night is bothering me, Megan."

She smiled. "It got me all bothered, too."

"No. I don't mean bothered as in hot and bothered. I mean bothered in the sense that I'm worried you may have gotten the wrong idea last night." He tried to keep his voice calm, reassuring. "I'm sorry if you did."

"The wrong idea?" She gave him a look that made it clear she knew he was a liar. Although her voice was steady and she didn't move a muscle, Chase knew she'd tensed.

He took a couple of steps forward until he stood directly in front of her. He started to put one hand on her shoulder for comfort but quickly decided he'd be much better off if he didn't touch Megan right now.

"I'm worried you got the wrong idea about that kiss," he said gently.

She shrugged. "I thought we agreed last night it wasn't much of a kiss anyway."

He wasn't going to get into that whole fish-sucking thing right now because both of them knew it wasn't true. The kiss had been hot.

"Megan, I'm sorry about last night. It shouldn't have happened."

Rather than appearing upset, she nodded thoughtfully. "No problem. Now if you want to come to my office, I'll get those papers for the carnival. Thanks for stopping by. Saves me coming out to your ranch. Anyway, these are lists of local companies, churches and organizations that may be interested in having booths at the carnival. I thought you and I could split the list and call around to see who wants to help."

She seemed so calm, so relaxed, but Chase knew she had to feel the sexual pull between them. Attraction crackled around them, and every time he looked into her wide green eyes, he had the almost overwhelming desire to do something unbelievably stupid. But hey, if she wanted to ignore what was happening, fine by him. He'd already done enough stupid things to last him a month. His gaze dropped to her lips. No, make that a year.

"Sure. Give me the lists. I'll call around," he said, anxious to get out of here.

She rewarded him with a smile. "Thank you." She headed to her office, but Chase waited where he was. No way was he going into that small room. He'd be all alone with Megan in a room that had a door and a wide, firm desk that would be perfect for making love on.

This cowboy was staying right where he was. After a minute or so, she came back carrying a handful of papers.

"Here you go," Megan said.

Chase took the lists and moved away from her, away from temptation. "Thanks. I'll let you know how I do."

She took two deliberate steps forward until she once again stood directly next to him. Then she patted his arm and said in a soothing voice, "It's going to be okay, Chase. Really it is."

He looked at her hand resting on his arm. He could imagine that same small hand wandering across his chest, her fingers caressing his skin. With effort, he swallowed past the knot in his throat.

"Don't worry so much," she said softly.

Then before he could do a single thing to stop her, she leaned up and placed a warm kiss on the side of his face. Every hormone in his body screamed for him to pull her into his arms and kiss her back, but he flat out wouldn't do it. He wasn't having sex with her no matter what she—and his own traitorous body—wanted.

Dagnabbit, he still had some scruples left. Granted, his supply was running low. But he still had a couple kicking around. And those scruples were going to see him through this debacle.

He gazed down into her wide green eyes, all set to tell her that he wasn't going to play, when she smiled at him. One of those purely feminine smiles that made a man's blood run hot and his IQ drop to that of fungus.

He only prayed that those couple of scruples he had left were going to be enough.

❧

"MAN ALIVE, THIS PLACE MAKES THE CITY DUMP LOOK like a tropical vacation spot," Chase muttered.

Megan glanced around the Honey City Park and sighed. Chase was right.

The two acres devoted to the children were barren and forlorn and contained more than a fair share of junk scattered around. As far as she could tell, the founding fathers of Honey had picked the ugliest piece of land to devote to the park.

In fact, even though most of Honey had lovely shade trees, this park was noticeably devoid of any trees. Well, there was one tired-looking pine that leaned at a precarious angle near the far corner of the park, but other than that, nothing. She couldn't help feeling sorry for the tree and even sorrier for what passed as playground equipment.

"The kids would be safer if they threw rocks at each other," Chase observed.

"It is rather bleak," she admitted. The few pieces of playground equipment that weren't broken were covered in a thick layer of dirt and rust.

"Bleak?" Chase walked farther into the park. "This place is pitiful. Downright pitiful. I didn't realize it was this bad."

Megan was glad he felt that way. She wanted Chase

to get as emotionally involved in this project as she was. Mostly for selfish reasons. Despite its appearance, this place meant a great deal to her. After her parents had died and she'd come to live with Aunt Florene in Honey, she'd spent many afternoons at the park. Florene hadn't wanted her around the house, and since she was new in town, she didn't have any friends. So, she'd hung around the park, and one fateful day, she'd met Chase Barrett there.

Tommy Whitman had started picking on her, shoving her and teasing her about not having parents. Then suddenly, Chase had appeared. Now as an adult, she knew he hadn't been the superhero she'd thought him to be that day, but to her, he'd always be a hero. Chase hadn't given an inch. He'd stood up to Tommy, something no one else in town wanted to do. Tommy had ended up backing down simply based on the look Chase had given him.

It had proven to be one heck of a look, since to this day Tommy still showed her respect whenever he saw her.

From the moment he'd stood up for her, Megan had been in love with Chase Barrett. And she still loved this park, but the children of this town deserved better. No matter what it took, she was going to make certain they got a great place to play.

She watched Chase head over to the playground equipment. Boy, it was good to see him. After their meeting at the library last week, Chase had avoided her, which wasn't an easy task considering how small Honey was. But Chase had pulled it off, which was one more indication of how rattled he was.

But now he'd had a few days to calm down. Hopefully he'd found a way to accept what had happened and had given up fussing about toothpicks.

"Megan, look at this." Chase shook one of the support poles for the swing set. The metal wobbled and let out an ominous creak. "This place is an ER nightmare. I think we need to call the city council tonight and tell them we're tearing this monster down right away."

Muttering and fussing, he moved over to the teeter-totter. When he pushed it, part of the seat came off in his hand. He turned to Megan, his expression dumbfounded. "I cannot believe this place."

"Now you see why I want to buy new equipment." She moved closer to him, drawn despite her promise to herself not to push him about their relationship. But how could she resist? He looked scrumptious today in jeans and a deep-burgundy T-shirt.

Trying to keep hold of her racing heart, she said, "I'll call Earl, although I know what he's going to say—the city doesn't have the manpower to take down this equipment."

Chase turned toward her, and for the first time since he'd arrived, he looked directly at her. His deep-blue gaze made tingles skitter across her skin.

"I have the manpower," he said. "I'll get my brothers over here tomorrow to tear this junk apart and gather up all the trash. I can use my truck to haul it to the dump."

"I can help, too."

He shook his head, causing a lock of his black hair to droop across his forehead. With an impatient gesture, he pushed it back in place. "Best not. If you're here, we can't cuss, and judging from what I see, this job will involve a lot of cussing."

She laughed. "I think I can stand a few choice words."

For long moments, he looked at her. She felt the same heat she always felt dance between them. Then Chase muttered something about scruples and not only looked away from her, but he also walked away from her.

Well, she wasn't going to let him get away so easily. She quickly caught up with him. "You're so nice," she told him. "This means a lot to the kids."

Her comment caused him to stop. He spun on his boot heel and faced her. Drat it all, he was frowning again.

"I'm not nice, Megan. Not at all."

"Sure, you are. You're concerned about children getting hurt on the playground."

He shook his head. "No. I'm worried about the city getting sued."

"Like I believe that. Admit it. You're worried about the children." He might want to paint himself as someone who didn't care, but she knew better. A man who didn't care wouldn't arrange to remove all the trash and dangerous equipment.

For a second, she thought he was going to argue with her, but then he sighed, the sound loud and heartfelt. "Let's walk this off and see how much space you have for new equipment."

Megan fell into step with him, knowing without a doubt what he was doing. Chase didn't want her complimenting him. He was obviously still upset by the kiss they'd shared.

That was a good sign, right?

Grabbing a pencil and notepad from her purse, she jotted down the rough measurements she and Chase came up with. There should be enough room to build a decent-size play area. The kids were going to go nuts when they saw it.

"At least you've got a flat piece of land. Should make it easier." Chase turned and headed over to the lone pine tree. "You going to cut this down?"

Horrified, Megan came to stand next to him. "Of course not. I wouldn't dream of hurting that poor tree." She patted the trunk. "It's earned the right to be part of the new park."

Chase chuckled. "Megan, it's a tree, not a war veteran. All it did was avoid tornadoes and snotty-nosed kids." He pointed toward a carving near the lower branches. "Looks like it didn't avoid all of those kids."

Megan moved to the side and studied the faded carving. A pair of initials surrounded by a heart. "That's so sweet."

"Bet the tree doesn't think so," Chase said dryly.

Turning, she studied him. "Probably not, but I think it's romantic that a couple was so in love that they carved their initials in the tree for everyone to see."

Chase made a snorting noise. "You can't be serious. This isn't about true love, Megan. Some lovestruck teenaged boy did that carving 'cause he was hoping to get lucky."

For one second, Megan wondered if Chase had been the wayward youth. She quickly rechecked the tree, happy to see the initials weren't his. Good. She didn't know what she would have done if the tree had been a testimony of Chase's love—or even lust—for another woman.

"I still think it's romantic," she maintained. "I think it would be wonderful to have someone so in love with me that he'd make that sort of public declaration. Imagine how special you'd feel, how treasured."

Chase moved closer, stopping when he stood only a few inches from her. Megan wished she knew what he was thinking, what he felt for her. He sure was frowning, so whatever he was thinking, he wasn't too happy about it.

Finally, he said, "You've always been special, Megan. I know maybe Florene didn't make you feel wanted, but the people of Honey care about you."

She had to smile at the vagueness of his comment. "The people care? What about you, Chase? Do you care? Am I special to you?"

"You know you are." He blew out a loud breath, and again, his gaze met hers. Attraction arced and sparkled between them, and even though she knew he wasn't a bit pleased about it, she also knew he could feel it, but he was fighting it.

"Dang it, Megan. This is all Leigh's fault. We were fine until she started all that naked business," he muttered.

Deciding she'd long since passed the point of pretending with Chase, she admitted, "It's not Leigh's fault. I've pictured you that way many times in my life. I've wanted you for a long time."

He groaned. "Someone must be putting pheromones in this town's water. That's all I've got to say."

"Why can't you accept what's happening between us?" she whispered. "Why can't you believe we can be much more than friends?"

They stood only a couple of inches apart, but now Chase closed that slim distance between them. He placed one hand under her chin and tilted her head so her gaze was locked with his. "I don't want to lose you in my life, Megan. That's how special you are to me." His deep-blue gaze scanned her face. "Don't you see that?"

"No," she said on a sigh. "Because the fact is you may lose me anyway. I can't help how I feel about you." When he opened his mouth to argue, she hurriedly added, "And it has nothing to do with Leigh. I've felt this way about you since the day you defended me against Tommy Whitman in this very park."

When the hand he'd used to tip her chin slid up the side of her face to caress her cheek, Megan pushed her advantage.

"Come on, cowboy. It won't kill you to admit you feel a little something for me," she teased, anxious to hear his response.

He studied her face for a heartbeat, then said, "Damn the scruples."

Before she could do much more than suck a startled breath into her lungs, he wrapped his arms around her, pulled her body flush against his own, and kissed her.

7

Chase knew he shouldn't be kissing Megan—that was the last thing he should be doing. Right now, he should be explaining how much her friendship meant to him. Barring that, he should be telling her how she'd always be a special part of his life.

He should be doing about any old blasted thing other than kissing Megan. But that's what he was doing —kissing her. And not just a nice little peck between friends. No, he was kissing her as if his life depended on it. One of those wild, wet, warm kisses that seemed to only lead to more kisses. Hungry kisses that spoke of lust and want and desire.

And Megan, bless her soul, was kissing him back with equal ferocity. He intended on breaking off the kiss. He really did. His brain kept sending signals to his lips to cut it out. But when she made a little mewing noise and wrapped herself even tighter around him, he cupped her face in his hands and deepened the kiss. At this point, he figured he'd already sunk the ship. He might as well capsize the dinghy, too.

So he gave in to the need he felt and kissed her. And kissed her. And kissed her.

The sound of a car backfiring somewhere nearby made reality crash back into him. His brain finally won the tug-of-war, and he tore his mouth free from Megan's.

He struggled to regain control, sucking deep breaths into his lungs. Of all the pea-brained moves. He was standing in the middle of a city park, in plain view of anyone who happened to drive by, kissing Megan. And not just kissing Megan, practically devouring her.

Way to solve the problem, Einstein. What had happened to his plan to once again calmly and rationally explain how they could never be more than friends? He'd decided over the past few days that if he explained his concerns to her often enough, she'd eventually come over to his way of thinking.

Of course, he might have had a better chance of convincing her of that little fact if he hadn't been busy kissing her. And what about his scruples? Plankton had more scruples than he did.

He slowly backed away from Megan. "About that kiss—"

After giving him a completely feminine smile that looked a little too complacent for his peace of mind, she held up one hand. "Don't tell me. It was a mistake, and it will never happen again."

Okay. At least she was being reasonable. "That's right."

"Got it. Well, you take care, Chase. I'll see you around."

With a flirty little wave, she walked away, leaving him standing in the middle of the park, dumbfounded. She couldn't seriously be okay with this, could she? Sure, he didn't want to hurt her. And sure, he knew sex would ruin their friendship, but how could she calmly walk away when two seconds ago they'd been sharing a kiss that had caught them both on fire?

He narrowed his gaze and watched her climb into her car. As she drove off, reality hit him in the face like a wet sock. She wasn't unaffected; she just wanted him to think she was. Megan didn't want to fight about the kiss, so she'd gone on the defensive and cut off any chance he had of starting a fight.

Smart lady. He couldn't help admiring the neat way she'd outmaneuvered him like a roper chasing a calf. Still, she might have avoided a fight today, but sooner or later, this mess was going to boil over. Megan still thought they had a romantic future, but they didn't.

Okay, after the two kisses they'd shared, he'd admit they shared more chemistry than he'd originally counted on. But chemistry could be ignored or even changed if you tried hard enough.

He blew out a disgusted breath and headed across the park to his truck. One way or the other, he needed to get her to face facts about their relationship.

"You stupid cowpoke, why don't you stop kissing her for starters," he muttered as he climbed in the cab of his truck.

Yeah, that would go a long way toward cooling things off.

꧁꧂

"THE COWARD'S HIDING FROM YOU," LEIGH SAID, then tossed a piece of popcorn into the air and caught it neatly in her mouth. "You need to stop him."

Megan scanned the carnival grounds, looking for Chase. Leigh was right. Chase was back to avoiding her. He'd done a lot of amazing footwork in the past few weeks to keep his distance, and she had no reason to expect him to change today.

His behavior was a direct result of their last kiss. She understood it had rattled him. It had rattled her, too. Heck, there was a fairly good chance it had registered on the Richter scale.

But rattled or not, she hadn't let the kiss distract her from the carnival and thankfully, neither had Chase. He'd simply used his brothers as a human shield.

The day after their last kiss when she'd swung by the park to help dismantle the old playground equipment at the appointed time of eight in the morning, she'd found Trent and Nathan standing in front of a neatly stacked pile of old rusty metal. They'd told her Chase had a conflict, so he and his brothers had started at six in the morning and were already done.

And gee, no one had thought to call her.

Then when she'd needed additional help lining up sponsors for the booths, Chase had done the calling, but Nathan had dropped the forms off at the library.

And when she'd run into trouble getting Earl to commit resources to assemble the tent, Chase had taken care of that as well. This time, though, Trent had been the one to drop off the final paperwork at the library.

She sighed. Nothing like running a committee with stand-ins.

"I still think you should give my idea a twirl," Leigh offered. "Whipped cream has brought many a man into line."

Megan continued to scan the crowd, still finding no sign of Chase. Disappointment washed over her, but she pushed it away. Today, she wasn't going to mope about Chase. The weather had turned out gorgeous, and the carnival had attracted a huge crowd. Not only did it appear most of Honey was crammed into the small city park, but quite a few out-of-towners had come as well.

"Are you sure Chase is here?" Megan asked Leigh, standing on her tiptoes to get a better look. "I need to talk to him about the auction."

"Yeah, he's here. Lurking around."

Well, that didn't make her feel any better. It hurt that Chase was avoiding her. She didn't enjoy feeling like day-old liver at a Sunday brunch.

Giving up, she turned and headed toward the tent where the auction would start in a few minutes. She'd just slipped inside the darkened interior when two of the men running some of the carnival games cornered her. As she'd feared, the bigger turnout was taking a toll on the homemade booths. They needed help making a few quick repairs.

Before Megan could even open her mouth, Chase spoke from behind her.

"I'll pitch in. Let me just grab my brothers, and I'll meet you over there."

After the men walked away, Megan turned to look at Chase. As usual, the sight of him made her heart beat faster.

"Hi," he said, moving a little closer when a large group of people came through the door.

Megan drank in the sight of him. He looked so handsome today in his jeans and plain white shirt. The simplicity of his clothes only served to showcase his gorgeous face and amazing blue eyes. Of course, she'd never tell him that. Chase Barrett was the least vain man she'd ever met. She knew his choice of clothing was based on practicality not on impression. But she was impressed, and she knew without even looking that the other women in the tent were impressed, too.

Slowly, she let her gaze wander over him. Her confidence soared when he took his time looking her over, too. She'd given a great deal of thought to her appearance, and the simple white sundress with the blue and green flowers made her feel pretty.

Chase seemed to agree because when he said, "You look nice," his voice had a husky overtone to it.

"Thanks. You look nice, too."

The goofy look Chase gave her made her laugh, and when he smiled in return, she felt her gloomy mood evaporate. Things were going to be fine. At least she hadn't lost her best friend. Not completely at least.

"I haven't seen you in forever," she said, even though she'd promised herself this morning that she wouldn't mention his absence. But how could she not? He really had been avoiding her.

"Yeah, sorry about that. I've been busy. But you got everything done you needed, right?"

She took a step closer to him. "Yes, but I still would've liked to have seen you."

"Couldn't be helped," was all he said.

"Really?" When he didn't elaborate, she pushed on. "Problems on the ranch?"

"Yes. No. Well, you know. Ranch stuff."

She smiled. "Ranch stuff?"

His shrug was self-conscious. "Horses, cows, ranch stuff."

Before Megan could question him further, Janet entered the tent, her red lips forming a wide smile at the sight of Chase. She was wearing her trademark flashy halter top, this time in the exact same shade of heart-attack red as her lipstick.

"Chase Barrett, you're harder to find than my ex-husband when he owes me alimony. I thought when I joined this committee that we'd spend time together. Maybe get to know each other."

Megan leaned forward and told the other woman, "Chase has been busy with ranch stuff."

Janet raised one thin brow. "Ranch stuff?"

Megan nodded and adopted her most sage voice. "Yes. You know, horses, cows, ranch stuff."

With a knowing nod, Janet said, "I see."

Megan bit back a giggle, and almost lost it completely when Chase groaned. "If you ladies will excuse me, I've got to go help fix a couple of the booths."

"Wait." Janet grabbed Chase's arm. "I just wanted you to know I plan on bidding on the trip to San Antonio. And if I win, I'll definitely need an escort."

With that and a quick wink, Janet wandered farther

into the tent, eventually sitting near the front with her girlfriends.

"Man, I'd forgotten all about that stupid trip." Chase moved closer to Megan. "Listen, you've got to make certain you come in with the winning bid."

"I will. I can go as high as five hundred dollars," she told him.

Chase frowned. "We already agreed to use my money, so I'll be the one to go as high as five hundred dollars."

Megan didn't want to argue with him, especially not in front of a large portion of Honey, so she merely nodded. Besides, if things got rough—and with Janet involved, they very well could—she could add her five hundred to his five hundred. There was no way Janet would bid more than a thousand dollars. Even she wasn't that crazy.

"Don't worry, I won't lose," Megan assured him.

His gaze locked with hers. "Truthfully, I'm not sure what worries me more—you losing or you winning."

While Megan turned his comment over in her mind, a commotion near the front of the tent drew her attention. The mayor was about to begin the auction. As much as she hated walking away from Chase when she'd finally gotten to see him, she had to go help with the auction.

"I have to go, but can I convince you not to disappear after the carnival is over?" Drat. She sounded as if she was pleading with him, which in a way, she was.

"I won't disappear," Chase assured her. "Besides, I have to find out who won the trip."

With that, he turned and left the tent. Megan felt

like the energy had left as well. But before she could even miss him, Earl called her to the podium.

Public speaking had never been her strong suit, but Megan figured after the past few weeks, she was definitely getting better at it. She made a few introductions, gave a lot of thanks and a couple of reminders, then stepped aside and let Earl start the auction.

Megan sat in a small chair next to Leigh and settled back to watch the action. The first few items were small: a suitcase and a silk flower arrangement. They attracted only a hundred dollars each. But as each minute ticked by, the items became more expensive. The laptop Nathan had donated generated a lot of bids, eventually selling for more than it would have if bought at retail.

"Jeez, this crowd is like a school of sharks smelling blood. Earl has whipped them into a frenzy," Leigh said.

Leigh was right. Earl had obviously missed his calling. The seventy-three-year-old mayor was teasing and cajoling the crowd out of money like an old pro. This could be bad. Very bad. Earl might very well convince the ladies of Honey that a trip with Chase was worth big bucks.

Megan glanced toward the back of the tent, hoping she'd spot Chase, but he wasn't there.

"Okay, next up is a trip to a bed and breakfast in San Antonio." Earl peered at the crowd over the top of his glasses. "Now, in case you folks don't know this, San Antonio isn't just famous for the Alamo. It's also one of the world's most romantic cities. And I understand that if a single lady bids, she can decide to ask Chase Barrett to come along with her for company. I want everyone here to picture yourself on the River Walk. Soft music. Fine wine. A full moon." After a long, long silence, he grinned a devil's grin. "May just have to bid on this myself and take Mrs. Guthrie there for our anniversary. This old house still has a fire burning in the hearth, if you know what I mean."

The crowd laughed, then Earl started the bidding at a hundred dollars. Before Megan could even raise her hand, the bid shot up to two-fifty.

"Oh, no, go find Chase," she whispered to Leigh.

Leigh glanced at her. "What's wrong?"

The bid went up to six hundred.

"Leigh, I only have a thousand dollars to bid on this. I promised Chase I'd make the winning bid."

The bid went to eleven hundred.

"Hurry," Megan told Leigh.

"I have fifteen hundred. Do I hear sixteen?" Earl asked.

"Wow, you'd think Chase was a professional gigolo the way these ladies are bidding," Leigh pointed out.

Megan felt her heart drop to her shoes. This bidding was out of control. By now, the only bidders were single women. All of the couples had long since dropped out. Megan grabbed Leigh's arm. "Seriously, you have to go get him."

"Two thousand dollars. I have two thousand dollars from Janet Defries," Earl said. "Come on, let's keep going. This is starting to get interesting." Megan felt her heart sputter. Oh, no. She stared at Leigh, who merely shrugged.

"Going once..."

"Going twice..."

Leigh shot to her feet. "Stop!"

The tent fell silent. Everyone stared at Leigh, who in turn stared at Megan. Leigh's expression clearly asked, "What do I do now?" but Megan had no answer for her.

"What's the problem?" Janet demanded. "I want to be declared the winner."

After a nerve-racking moment, Leigh turned toward Janet. "Tell me something. If you win, are you going to expect Chase to come with you on this trip?"

Janet's smile was feline. "I might like some company."

"Oh." Leigh looked at Megan, then turned toward Earl. "In that case, I think everyone here should know something."

"And what would that be, Leigh?" Earl asked patiently.

"Um, well...Janet can't win the trip because Chase can't go with her," Leigh said.

Megan frowned. Where was she going with this?

"Chase promised he would," Janet pointed out, her temper obviously at the breaking point.

Leigh grinned, a self-satisfied grin that Megan knew beyond a doubt boded trouble. She braced herself.

"Well, Janet, Chase made that promise a while ago," Leigh said. "Before he and Megan became engaged."

8

"**C**ongratulations, Chase. Good for you."

Puzzled, Chase stopped hammering the side of the Go Fish booth back together and turned to look at the couple standing next to him. Edith and George Brown, owners of a neighboring ranch, both grinned at him.

"Um, thanks. But Megan arranged everything. I just did what she told me to do," Chase admitted, not wanting anyone to think he had anything to do with the success of the carnival and auction. Megan deserved all the credit.

The Browns laughed, and George slapped him on the back. "Son, that's the best way to handle things. Just do what Megan tells you to do. You'll be a much happier man."

Still laughing, the elderly couple wandered away, leaving Chase frowning after them. What had George meant by that last comment?

Shaking his head, he went back to work, quickly

fixing the booth and letting the juvenile fishers return to their fun.

Once he finished all the necessary repairs, he cut back toward the auction tent. Every few feet, someone stopped him with congratulations. After the third time, a bad feeling settled in his stomach. That feeling only intensified when he saw Leigh racing toward him, Nathan on her heels.

"Hey, Chase," Leigh said when she skidded to a stop in front of him.

Her expression screamed guilt.

"What did you do?" Chase asked, knowing he really didn't want to hear her answer.

"See, there was a bit of a problem during the auction." She fidgeted with her necklace that said: Kiss Me, You Frog.

"I'll say," Nathan muttered. "Tell him, Leigh."

Chase put his hand on his sister's arm. "Yeah, tell me, Leigh. Right this second."

She let go of her necklace and put her hands on her hips. "Fine. But it's not a big deal. All that happened was I told some of the people at the auction that you and Megan are engaged."

Chase felt like his blood turned icy cold. For a minute, he only stared at his sister, unable to believe what she'd just told him. Then he got angry.

"Why in the blazes would you say something like that?" he demanded.

Leigh shrugged. "The bidding on that trip got out of hand, and Megan didn't have enough money. When it became obvious Janet Defries was going to win, I stopped the auction and said you couldn't go on the trip with Janet because you're engaged to Megan." She smiled brightly. "So now that you're up-to-date, I'm heading on over to the—"

Chase silenced her with a frown. Then he looked at Nathan. "Did you say anything to clear up this mess?"

"Me?" Nathan shook his head slowly. "I didn't have a chance. Before I knew what had happened, Leigh said I'd donate the two thousand dollars the town would have made if Janet's bid had been accepted."

Unable to believe what she'd done, Chase stared at his sister. "You're like a one-person wrecking crew today."

Rather than appearing insulted, Leigh said, "Just trying to help."

"Help isn't the four-letter word I'd associate with you, Leigh," Chase muttered, heading toward the tent. As he grew nearer, more and more people congratulated him on his engagement to Megan. He'd have to set a lot of people straight later today, but right now, he had to see Megan.

He found her at the front of the auction tent, trying to talk to Earl and a couple of members of the city council. Not unexpectedly, no one was listening to her. They were too busy telling each other that they'd known all along that he and Megan were more than just friends.

When he stopped next to her, Megan looked up, relief immediately crossing her face. "I can't believe Leigh did this," she said. "Earl, Chase is here now. He and I want to explain that Leigh was wrong to—"

"Steal your thunder." Earl patted Megan's arm "I know. You and Chase probably wanted to wait before making an announcement. But don't worry, we won't push you for a wedding date. At least not right away."

"Still, they shouldn't wait too long if they want to reserve the church for the wedding." This came from Trent, who had come up to the group and now stood grinning at Megan and Chase like a court jester. "You two lovebirds don't want to let the grass grow beneath your feet. Seize the day, I say. You may want to give some thought to hightailing it to Las Vegas and getting hitched right away."

"Cute," Chase said to his younger brother. Turning back to the group, he said, "Could Megan and I have a minute with Earl, folks?"

The crowd agreed and after a few more congratulations, left them alone with the mayor.

Chase studied Megan's face, debating how to handle this fiasco. Although he knew she wanted their relationship to move into the romantic arena, he also knew she'd never push him into marriage. She didn't seem any more pleased about this bogus story than he was.

"Earl, about what Leigh said. She was wrong," Chase said, wanting to flatten this problem quickly.

His tone must have convinced Earl that he was serious. The mayor slipped his glasses down his nose and studied Chase and Megan closely. Finally, he asked Megan, "Is that the truth? Is Leigh wrong?"

Megan didn't hesitate. "Yes, she's wrong."

"I see." Earl pushed his glasses back in place.

Megan shifted her weight, anxiously gnawing her bottom lip.

Earl scratched his head. "Well, I'm not sure I

completely understand what the two of you are telling me."

"Leigh got it wrong," Chase reiterated.

"Do you mean Leigh is wrong about you getting married anytime soon? I'd say that was your own business. But if, for instance of course, you were to tell me that you're not engaged after all, then we'd have a real problem on our hands..."

"Um...problem?"

"For starters, that would mean Janet is the rightful winner of the trip. And Chase did agree to go with the winner if asked, so we'd need him to take Janet to San Antonio."

"Oh."

"Then there's the embarrassment factor. Not only would you two look like fools, but everyone might wonder if the auction was legit. Could cause the city big problems."

Chase gulped.

Earl turned to Megan, his stare intense. "I sure would hate to see a black cloud settle over this great carnival and auction you arranged. But if Leigh was wrong, then I guess Leigh was wrong."

Chase heard Megan groan softly by his side, and he felt like kicking his family tree. Earl was right. If they turned around now and said Leigh had been joking, then Megan's hard work might fall under suspicion. Sure, they could explain it, but some people would never believe them.

Megan took off her glasses. "Leigh was wrong about—"

"The wedding," Chase said. "We're not planning on

getting married anytime soon. We want to have a long engagement."

She'd been all set to confess to the mayor, and he couldn't let her do it. They could work this out with a little time. It wouldn't kill him to pretend to be engaged to Megan for a few weeks.

Then, once things died down and her plans for the park were firm, they could tell everyone the engagement was off because they'd decided they made better friends than lovers. No one would be harmed by the deception, and the kids would still get their playground.

He looked at Megan, who was obviously confused by what he'd told Earl. He explained to the mayor, "We're planning a long engagement. And don't try to change our minds about this. We both need time to think about our future."

As much as he hated lying to Earl, he knew he was doing the right thing for Megan and the town. He'd simply have to bide his time until they could straighten this out. But when he got home, he and Leigh were going to have a long, hard talk.

"Good. Good. Glad to hear that was what you wanted to tell me." Earl leaned forward and placed a kiss on Megan's cheek. "I'm really happy for you, honey. Despite his ornery tendencies, Chase here is a good man."

Beside him, Chase could feel how tense Megan was. Wanting to lighten the mood, he said to Earl, "Ornery tendencies? I don't have anything but pure sugar pumping through my veins."

Earl snorted. "You're a hoot, boy. A real hoot." With

that he walked away, leaving Megan and Chase alone at the far end of the tent.

"Why didn't you tell him the truth?" Megan whispered.

Chase shrugged. "Because I don't want it to spoil the auction."

"But we're lying. We're not engaged."

That part bothered him, too. "Megan, will you marry me?"

She blinked. "What?"

"Now when people ask you if I really proposed, you can truthfully say yes," he pointed out.

Catching on quickly, Megan smiled. "I get it, and my answer is yes. Now you can tell everyone I accepted."

For a heartbeat, they shared a smile, two old friends who had figured out a solution to a major problem. Then worry gnawed at him. What if she'd misunderstood? "But you know this engagement is—"

"Relax; I'm not taking it seriously."

"Good. After the trip, we'll announce we've broken up."

"Are you sure you want to go on that trip together? I'll understand if you'd rather not."

Chase studied her, standing in front of him in her pretty white sundress, her hair fluffed around her face. She looked sexy and sweet at the same time. As far as he could tell, the two of them going away together on that trip was a lousy idea. But as Megan continued to look at him, the words dried up on his lips. He couldn't let the people in this town think he'd dumped her. And that's exactly what they'd think if he didn't go to San Antonio with Megan.

Concern for her feelings forced him to add, "But, Megan, we're going on this trip as friends. That's all."

"I understand." She drew an imaginary X across her chest. "I promise I won't kiss you. Nor will I picture you naked. I will be on my very best behavior."

Chase knew she meant that. Megan sincerely intended on being on her best behavior.

Now if only he could say the same thing about himself.

છ૪ઝ

"I SHOULD HAVE GUESSED YOU AND CHASE WERE IN love," Amanda Newman said the following Tuesday when she pushed her cart into line behind Megan at Palmer's Grocery. "The way you looked at each other the night of the meeting made it clear you both cared deeply."

Megan had been putting her groceries on the conveyor belt, but she stopped and turned to look at the minister's wife. Sure, there was a chance Amanda had seen something in her gaze as she'd looked at Chase.

She was, after all, in love with the man. But Chase didn't love her. At least, he didn't romantically love her —or so he said.

Not yet anyway. But Megan still had hope. He had agreed to keep up their pretend engagement. A man didn't do that for just any woman who crossed his path.

"So, you saw something in the way Chase looked at me?" Megan couldn't resist asking Amanda.

"Oh, yes. He looked at you the same way Conrad

looks at me." Amanda's expression turned blissful. "Like you make him complete."

Megan liked the thought that in some way, Chase might feel she made him complete. "And he looked at me that way?"

Amanda laughed. "Of course he did, dear. Why else would he want to marry you?"

The comment felt like a bucket of ice water poured over Megan's head. That was the problem—their engagement wasn't real. Moreover, according to him, they would never be anything more than friends. Of course, friends didn't kiss the way she and Chase did.

"If you don't finish putting your groceries on the counter, I'm going to have to arrest you for loitering."

At Trent's voice, Megan turned. He stood at the end of the counter, his grin wild and wicked. Holding up a head of lettuce, he asked, "You gonna make dinner for your loving fiancé?"

Megan shot Trent a reproachful look because he knew all too well that the engagement wasn't real. But her look only made him laugh.

He tossed the head of lettuce from hand to hand. "If you are, I should warn you that Chase is more of a meat and potatoes guy. He likes salads, but not as the main course." Nodding toward her cart, he added, "Why don't you give the rest of the folks standing in line a break and finish emptying your cart. I'll bag for you."

Megan glanced behind her and realized with a start she really was holding up the line.

"Sorry," she said and quickly loaded her remaining food on the counter.

"She just got engaged," Amanda explained to the

99

other customers in line. "It's to be expected that she'd be distracted. All those wedding plans to make."

"When's the big day?" Peggy Turner, the cashier, asked.

"Yeah, Megan, when's the big day?" Trent winked. "I want to be certain I mark it on my calendar."

Megan felt the warmth of a blush climb her face. She hated lying with a passion, but she also agreed with Chase. The best way to handle this situation was to wait a few weeks, then tell everyone that she and Chase had decided they made better friends than lovers.

But she couldn't help wishing they really were engaged. Whenever someone asked her when the wedding was, her heart did a little flutter, almost as if she were really marrying Chase.

Everyone was looking at her, so Megan gave them the pat answer she and Chase had developed for when they were confronted with this question. "We want to have a long engagement, so we haven't set a date yet."

"Why a long engagement?" Amanda asked. "You've known each other for most of your lives." Before Megan could respond, she pressed on. "If you want to have a June wedding, you need to hurry."

Megan grabbed on to that excuse with relief. "Yes. That's it. I want to have a June wedding, and since it's already May, I don't have time to put something together on such short notice. I want to wait until June of next year so I can have the wedding of my dreams."

Her answer must have sounded pretty good because Amanda's expression softened. "You do that. It's impor-tant that your wedding be exactly right."

Feeling satisfied that she'd handled this situation

well, Megan paid the cashier and helped Trent finish bagging her groceries. Again, she couldn't help wishing her engagement were real. She really would like a June or September wedding. While she was too late for June, she certainly could put together a wonderful ceremony before September. That is, naturally, if she could convince the groom to actually be a groom.

Just when Megan thought she was going to escape the store without future incidents, Trent said, "I don't think you should wait a whole year. What's important is you're getting married. You shouldn't care where or when the ceremony takes place."

Megan walked over to him and said softly, "Cut it out."

But Trent seemed to be warming to the topic. "Chase has been on his own for long enough. I bet the ladies of this town would be more than happy to help you come up with a beautiful wedding that could be pulled together quickly."

"Oh, yes," Amanda said. "I'm sure Conrad would be able to find time for you. And if you want an outdoor ceremony, it's always lovely out at the lake. Or better yet, hold it at Chase's ranch. It would be wonderful by the pool."

Megan debated her answer and finally decided to use her groceries as an excuse to escape. "I'll keep all those ideas in mind. Thank you."

Then before anyone else could come up with suggestions for a wedding that realistically would never happen, Megan pushed her cart toward the parking lot. As she expected, Trent fell into step next to her.

"You're an evil man," she told him as soon as they

were out of earshot of anyone else. "You shouldn't tease me like that. I don't want anyone to find out that the engagement isn't real."

Trent shrugged. "Maybe I wasn't teasing you. Maybe I don't think you and Chase should break your engagement even if it is fake."

They had reached her car, so Megan turned to face him. She'd never had a serious conversation in her life with Chase's carefree younger brother. But his expression told her he was absolutely sincere today.

"You really feel that way?" she asked.

"Sure," Trent said. "I think you're good for Chase. You always have been. Marriage would probably suit him."

Megan stared at Trent, stunned that he could feel that way. She thought he, of all people, would discourage his oldest brother from marriage. She'd never figured him for an ally.

"You're teasing me again, right?" she asked, deciding this was simply another one of his pranks.

Trent shook his head. "No. Dead serious this time. I love Chase. I want what's best for him, even if sometimes he's too dense to know what that might be. Sure, at first it was a joke, but now that I've thought about it, I think you two are perfect together."

Working on autopilot, Megan unlocked her car and loaded her groceries inside. Periodically, she glanced at Trent, who was helping her. Trent thought she and Chase were perfect together? Would wonders never cease?

After her groceries were in the car, she faced Trent again. "I guess Leigh told you how I feel about Chase."

"Leigh didn't have to tell me. It's always been written all over you. Chase is the only one who never noticed," Trent said.

"I'm that obvious, huh?"

Trent pulled his sunglasses out of his shirt pocket and slipped them on. "Oh, yeah. You're like a neon sign. But hey, that's good. You should let people know how you feel about them. Life's too short to waste time playing games."

Megan laughed. "This from you? The master at playing games?"

"See, now that's where you're wrong. I'm always painfully honest with the ladies I date. They know up front that we're only having fun."

Megan slipped her keys into the pocket of her slacks. "Thanks for telling me you'd think I'd be good for Chase. I think so, too. But he has to do what he feels is right for him. I can't force him to fall in love with me."

Trent leaned against her car, his mouth thoughtful. "I don't agree. I think Chase needs encouragement. He's spent most of his life believing that love doesn't exist. You should take whatever drastic measures are necessary."

Uh-oh. She'd heard this sort of thing before. This could be dangerous. Especially to Chase. "What exactly do you mean by drastic measures?"

"You've got resources on your side, Megan. You should use them."

Totally baffled, she asked, "What resources?"

"Leigh. Me. Nathan. We can work on Chase from the inside while you work on him from the outside."

Oh, no. The thought of Trent, Leigh, and Nathan ganging up on Chase was positively scary.

"Chase needs to make this decision on his own," Megan said firmly. "I appreciate your offer, but this is between the two of us."

For a few seconds, Trent simply grinned. "Megan, I have an idea. Get yourself some racy undies. Maybe in red. Then drive out to the ranch, knock on the door, and when Chase answers—"

Megan groaned. Did all these Barretts think alike? "I know, flash him my scanty undies and a couple of cans of whipped cream and tell him I'm dessert. Leigh already suggested that one."

Trent seemed puzzled. "Wow, Megan, I wasn't going to say anything like that. The racy undies were to go under your clothes, of course. They would give you self-confidence when you went to talk to Chase about making this engagement real. I saw a show on TV where the lady said she always felt like she could conquer the world when she wore her sexiest underwear under her suit." He gave her his best chief of police look. "You and Leigh sure come up with some wild stuff. Whipped cream. Yow."

Closing her eyes, Megan willed herself not to blush but failed. She felt warmth climb her face. When she finally looked at Trent again, he was grinning.

"Thank you for the suggestion," she said stiffly. "I'll consider it."

"Not that Chase wouldn't like the whipped cream thing. I'm sure he would." He tipped his head, lowered his sunglasses and studied her. "You wouldn't by any chance be able to tie a cherry stem into a knot using only your tongue, would you?"

Her voice was strangled when she said, "Um, I'm pretty sure that's a talent I lack."

Trent seemed unaware of her discomfort "Oh, it's real easy. You just need to practice. First, you get yourself some cherries. Then you—"

Megan held up one hand to silence him. "Thanks, but I'm not really interested in learning how to tie cherry stems with my tongue."

"Too bad. Because if you did that whipped cream thing and could also tie a cherry stem, I'm pretty sure Chase would follow you straight to the altar without making a single protest."

Shaking her head at Trent's nonsense, Megan opened her car door. "I'll keep the suggestion in mind. But please, let me work this out with Chase myself."

With a shrug, Trent said, "You bet. I won't interfere. Not a bit. Just wanted you to know you've got friends on your side."

Because she knew in his own way, Trent's offer of help was sincere, Megan said, "Thanks."

"No problem..." His voice drifted away as Lucy Marshall, a recent divorcee, walked by carrying a tiny bag of groceries. She gave Trent a flirty smile.

"Hey there, Trent," Lucy said.

Trent moved forward. "Hey, Lucy. Let me give you a hand carrying those groceries." He took two more steps forward before stopping and glancing back at Megan. "We're done, right?"

Megan bit back a smile. Trent was in full wolf mode. "Yes, we're done. See you around."

Trent nodded, but his attention was already riveted on Lucy. As Megan climbed into her car, she watched Trent flirt with the other woman. And Lucy flirted back. Outrageously. Now why couldn't she be like those two? Why couldn't she go after what she wanted with gusto? Sure, she'd been fairly direct with Chase the past few weeks, but still, it didn't seem to be enough. She needed to think of another way to get him to see her as the woman she really was, not just as a friend he'd known for twenty years.

Megan sat for a minute, watching Trent and Lucy until they walked away. Then with a sigh, she started her car and had just put it in Reverse when she stopped.

Drop by precious drop, her common sense left her. When it was completely gone, she carefully put the car back in Park, turned it off, climbed out, and locked the door. Then she headed across the parking lot toward the entrance to the grocery store.

She suddenly had the urge to buy some whipped cream and cherries.

✂ 9 ✂

"I'm having a wonderful time. How about you?" Megan asked.

Chase gripped the steering wheel tighter. They were two hours into the drive to San Antonio with another hour plus left to go.

Was he having a wonderful time? Was it possible to have a wonderful time while simultaneously feeling like a captain who knew in his bones that his ship was going to sink?

Wonderful wasn't exactly the word he'd choose to describe this afternoon. Uncomfortable as hell seemed to sum it up nicely. He could count on one hand the number of times he'd felt this uncomfortable.

There was the night of his eighteenth birthday when his high school math teacher had made a pass at him. And the time he'd broken up with a woman only to serve as best man at her wedding three weeks later when she'd married a friend of his.

Neither of those times came close to being stuck in

the tiny cab of his truck with Megan. Of course, she'd been nothing but nice and thoughtful. Megan specialized in nice and thoughtful.

But she'd talked pretty much nonstop since he'd picked her up at two o'clock this afternoon. She'd talked about the weather, and the new playground equipment she'd ordered, and some recent acquisitions the library had made.

But she'd never mentioned their last kiss or the sham engagement, which was driving him nuts.

"Chase, you didn't answer me. Are you having a good time?"

"Yeah. Just swell." Noticing a billboard for a gas station at the next exit, he decided now would be a really good time for a break. "I need to get gas."

Not surprisingly, Megan agreed. She's been agreeing with everything this afternoon. "Sounds good."

After a few minutes, Chase pulled up next to a pump and turned off the engine. He looked over at Megan, who smiled at him.

Damn. He felt like a jackass.

Megan was being sweet, and he was as snarly as a bear woken up from his winter nap. But how else was he supposed to behave when he had to spend the weekend trying to resist Megan? After the two fiery kisses they'd shared, he knew it wasn't going to be easy.

"I'm going to go inside and buy a soda," Megan said. "Want anything?"

His sanity? His peace of mind? His old life back? He shook his head. "No. I'm fine."

But as he filled the tank on his truck, he realized he hadn't been fine since that night at the city council meeting. Ever since then, he'd been fighting Megan and himself. And now, after the auction, he was fighting most of the town. Everywhere he went these days, people told him how perfect he and Megan were for each other.

Except for one tiny fact—she believed in love and marriage, and he knew those two concepts were a sham. He cared enough about Megan to refuse to be the man who broke her heart.

Megan still hadn't returned when he finished pumping the gas, so he headed inside the convenience store to make sure she was okay. He found her standing near the register and started toward her when he noticed she was talking to the man in line behind her.

No, she was flirting with the man in line behind her. Or at least, she wasn't doing a damn thing to stop the guy from flirting with her. And the man was flirting with Megan, at least he was when he wasn't too busy checking her out. The sight of the two of them smiling and laughing stopped Chase dead in his tracks.

As he watched, the yahoo leaned closer to Megan and asked, "You live around here?"

Megan gave the man a vague smile and Chase's self-control snapped like a twig. What the blazes was she doing? She was an engaged woman, for crying out loud. She couldn't flirt with other men.

Struggling to keep a tight rein on his temper, Chase crossed the store at a clip and slipped one arm around Megan's waist.

"There you are, darlin'," he said, and with a pointed look at the yahoo, dipped his head, and kissed Megan soundly.

He'd only meant for the kiss to make his position clear, but once his lips touched Megan's, he got distracted. He deepened the kiss, and by the time he lifted his head, both of them were breathing hard.

Megan stared up at him and blinked. "Why did you do that?"

He didn't answer her because he wasn't sure what the answer was. Instead, he turned his attention back to the man standing behind Megan. "My fiancée doesn't live around here. She lives in Honey, with me."

That shut the yahoo up. Up close, Chase realized the other man was younger, maybe in his early twenties. But being young was no excuse for poaching on another man's woman. The kid took a couple of steps back, apparently catching on.

Satisfied that the situation was now clear, Chase looked at Megan. She continued staring at him as if he'd lost his mind, and it hit him like a kick in the head from an angry horse—he'd just acted like a real fiancé.

Ah, hell. Now he was getting as crazy as the rest of Honey.

Megan was still staring at him as she paid for her soda, then led the way back to the truck. They both climbed in without comment, and Chase headed back toward the interstate. He knew Megan was waiting for him to say something, to offer some explanation for his behavior. But truthfully, he had none.

Finally, he said, "Sorry about what happened back there."

"What exactly did happen back there? I'm a little confused."

Chase glanced at her, then returned his attention to

the road. "I didn't like the way that man was treating you, so it seemed the easiest way to solve the problem."

Even to him, the explanation seemed lame. But hey, that was his story, and he was sticking to it.

Megan had turned toward him as much as her seat belt would let her. "He wasn't doing anything, Chase. Just being nice."

"Nice my as——" He cleared his throat, still struggling to understand why he was so upset. "That man was coming on to you because he wanted you. Who knows what would've happened if I hadn't come inside the store?"

His outburst startled both of them. Whoa. He was acting like a jealous lover. What in the name of sweet sanity was wrong with him? Megan was his friend. If she wanted to flirt with yahoos, then that was her business.

The only problem was his mind might be convinced it wasn't his business, but he couldn't seem to get his emotions wrapped around the concept.

"Chase, were you jealous?" Megan asked softly.

When he cut his glance her way, she had a warm, sweet smile on her face.

Oh, for the love of Pete. He kept making this situation worse and worse. "No, I wasn't jealous. Just concerned for your safety."

For a heartbeat, Megan simply studied him. Then an almost blissful expression crossed her face.

"Thank you for your concern," she said.

Chase felt like a man knitting his own noose. "Megan, I only said you were my fiancée because it was the easiest way to get the guy to back off." Some ornery part of his makeup compelled him to add, "Course it didn't help that you were flirting with him."

"Flirting? I wasn't flirting with him. He asked me how to get to San Antonio, and I gave him directions."

Chase snorted. "There are about thirty signs pointing the way to San Antonio. He needed directions about as much as I need to shave my legs."

She narrowed her eyes. "Be that as it may, that's what he asked me. I was merely being helpful. And he wasn't flirting with me."

Yeah, right, and cowboys don't love horses. "Don't be naive, Megan. That man was hot for you."

"How do you know?"

"Because of the way he looked at you," Chase managed to say, still steaming at the thought of that guy checking out Megan when she wasn't looking. Not that Megan wasn't worth checking out. She looked especially pretty today in her jeans and pink T-shirt. The clothes showed off her trim figure but were completely respectable.

Megan frowned at him. "How exactly did he look at me?"

Chase rolled his shoulders, trying to ease the knot forming in his muscles. "Like he was picturing you naked."

With a laugh, Megan placed one hand on his arm. "Oh, right. You're teasing me. For a second there I was worried you were really upset. I should have known better. You'd never get jealous of a man talking to me. Like you keep saying, we're friends, nothing more. What's to get jealous of?"

Nothing irked him more than having his own words

tossed back at him, but Megan had a point. They were friends, and he had no cause to be jealous.

Reaching over, he turned on the radio, making the music a tad louder than was really necessary. But the volume forced them to stop talking, which made him want to shout hallelujah. As far as he was concerned, he was through talking for today. Maybe for the rest of the trip.

Because it seemed whenever he opened his mouth these days, he got himself in trouble.

❧

"You have to be wrong," Megan said, leaning farther over the counter. "Please check your computer again."

Judy Sullivan, Amanda Newman's sister and the owner of the B&B, shook her head. "I'm sorry about this mix-up, but I got a call yesterday from a woman saying she was Megan Kendall—saying she was you. She explained that she and Mr. Barrett were engaged and would only require one room. Since this is a busy time of year, I naturally was happy to have an additional room to rent out." She studied Megan. "My sister told me a couple of days ago about your engagement. Congratulations, by the way."

Megan forced herself to smile. "Thanks." Next to her, she could feel tension radiating from Chase. After Judy checked them in and gave them a key to their mutual room, Megan picked up her small suitcase and cosmetic case and finally gathered the courage to look at him.

"I don't know what happened," she told Chase. "I didn't call here."

"I know. Considering the way things have been going, we should have expected this. If I had to bet, I'd say this was another case of Leigh playing the two of us like a fiddle." He reached out and took Megan's suitcase, then nodded his head toward the stairs. "There doesn't seem to be anything we can do about it right now. Let's just hope this is a big room with two double beds."

Megan appreciated Chase being a good sport, but she knew deep down he was upset. She was upset, too. She didn't want Chase to think she'd planned this as a way to seduce him. He'd been nice enough to help with the fundraiser, and even though their personal relationship wasn't developing as she'd hoped, she also respected him enough not to trick him.

Of course, ever since the kiss at the gas station, she couldn't help wondering if Chase's feelings toward her were starting to change.

He'd kissed her like a jealous man, and then he'd acted even more like a jealous man when they'd discussed it in the car. A friend wouldn't have cared that someone else was flirting with her.

But a man falling in love would care a lot. Feeling infinitely better, Megan unlocked the door to the room and walked inside. A huge, king-size bed took up almost all the room. The bed was gorgeous, covered with a delicate flowered spread that coordinated with the drapes. Besides the bed, there was a small chair in the corner and a dresser.

But mostly, the room was just bed.

"I don't believe this," Chase muttered over Megan's shoulder. "This is insane."

He set the suitcases down, then walked out of the room. Megan heard him heading back downstairs, and she didn't need to be clairvoyant to know he was trying to get them a different room. She couldn't blame him. Despite the sedate, refined decorations of the room, it did fairly scream sex. Okay, sedate, refined sex, but sex nonetheless. The bed was the focal point, and there was no way not to stare at it.

After a few minutes, a dejected Chase walked into the room. "I know this isn't going to be a surprise to you, but this room—which is the bridal suite, by the way—is the only room available tonight. Now who would have seen that coming?" Sarcasm dripped from his voice.

"I'm sorry," Megan said, meaning it.

Chase gave her a rueful smile. "Don't be. This isn't your fault. My sister did this, probably with the help of my brothers. When I get back to Honey, I'm finding a new family."

"We can go to another hotel," she offered.

He sat in the small chair in the corner, then frowned at the bed. "No. That would hurt Amanda's feelings. We can stay here tonight. I'll sleep on the floor."

Megan glanced around. Since the bed was so big, there wasn't a lot of floor space to be had. But she didn't point this out to Chase. She also knew better than to argue with him as to which one of them slept on the bed.

She set her suitcase on the bed and opened it. Her pink nightie was folded neatly on top.

Chase groaned. "Megan, we have to have some rules if we're going to share this room tonight. For starters, I'm not going to have sex with you. Nothing personal, of course, but that's the way it's going to be."

Biting back her smile took a little effort. "I understand."

He waved at her suitcase. "Second, we're both sleeping in our clothes. You can't run around this room in your nightgown or your underwear or your robe. You must have clothes on at all times." Containing her amusement was getting more and more difficult, but she knew Chase was serious, so she did her best to keep her expression neutral.

"Okay," she said. "I promise to keep my clothes on at all times." He looked so unhappy that she walked over and patted his shoulder. "I'll do whatever it takes so you can enjoy this trip. I'm not trying to trick or seduce you, Chase. I'll admit, I'd like our relationship to be different, but I know you don't feel the same way."

Even saying those words hurt, but she meant what she said. She wanted him to be happy, even if that meant he might never return her love.

Chase looked at her, his expression resigned. "Megan, I care enough about you not to want to see you hurt. But I'm having one hell of a time fighting you, my family, plus the entire town of Honey. A man's only got so much self-control, and mine's running out."

Her heart fluttered a little at his confession. Chase wasn't immune to her; he was just worried about her. But he also felt the simmering sexuality dancing between them.

Still, Megan had no intention of using that knowledge against Chase. As much as she wanted them to be lovers, she accepted that he didn't.

"Let's get out of here," she suggested. "We'll go explore and have dinner somewhere."

For a second, Megan thought Chase was going to argue, but then with a sigh, he stood and nodded toward the door. "Lead on. The way my day is going, I'd probably choose a restaurant that only serves oysters."

C hase had never slept on a bed of nails, but he'd be willing to bet his favorite bull that it was more comfortable than the floor in their hotel room. For the hundredth time, he rolled over, trying to find a comfortable position. But it just didn't exist. The floor was tougher than the rockiest Texas ground.

"Why don't you come join me in this soft bed?" Megan's voice drifted down around Chase like a siren's song.

Oh, no, she wasn't tempting him now. Not with a soft bed and an even softer body. No, sir. He'd withstood so much already. He could make it through the night without making love to her. He was strong.

Sort of.

"Thanks, but I'm fine down here," he lied. "You go on to sleep."

"I can't. I feel terrible that you're stuck on the floor. Here you were so nice to agree to come on this trip with the winner of the auction, and now you end up sleeping on the floor. The guilt is killing me. Besides, this is silly. We're mature adults. We can share a bed without having sex."

Chase didn't mean to laugh, but he couldn't help himself. "No, I don't think we could."

Her voice was indignant when she said, "You really can trust me. Just because I have feelings for you that are more than those of a friend doesn't mean you can't trust me. I promise I won't try to seduce you."

Yeah, but if he got in that bed, he'd have to resist two people—Megan and himself. Ticking him off big-time was the fact that most of his body thought sleeping with Megan was a dandy idea. The only organ holding out on the plan was his brain. Okay, and maybe his heart. But that added up to slim defenses if his libido decided to get rowdy during the night.

No, the smart move was to remain where he was. On the blasted floor in this stupid room.

"Chase, you didn't answer me. I said I promise I won't seduce you. Please get off the floor and come to bed. I'll stay on my side. You won't even know I'm here."

"Yeah, I will."

"No. I promise. I won't come anywhere near you. I'll be good."

See now, that was the problem. Most of him didn't want her to be good. Most of him was rooting for her to be very, very bad. As far as he was concerned, there wasn't a bed in the world wide enough for the two of them to sleep in.

"Thanks, Megan, but I'm going to stay here." He

rolled over onto his side and closed his eyes, praying for sleep.

After a couple of seconds, a soft shuffling sound made him turn onto his back. In the faint light drifting in from the partially opened drapes, Chase saw that to his horror, Megan was sliding off the side of the bed. He jackknifed into a sitting position.

"Dang, Megan, what are you doing?"

"It's not fair that you sleep on the floor. Since you won't sleep on the bed, I'm joining you on the floor," she said, dropping her pillow next to his. "Scoot over. The bed takes up so much space there's not much room here on the floor."

Chase felt as if he'd forgotten how to breathe. For a couple of seconds, he watched her, dumbfounded, while she fluffed her pillow and pulled the blanket off the bed.

"Now there, isn't this better?" she asked. "Come on. Stretch out and close your eyes. We need to go to sleep."

He finally recovered from his shock enough to tell her, "This isn't going to work. If I'm not willing to make love to you on the bed, I'm sure not going to make love to you on the floor."

Although, as much as he hated himself for it, he really, really wanted to. She smelled wonderful and looked tempting as sin curled on the floor, smiling up at him.

"I already gave you my promise that I wouldn't seduce you. Now let's go to sleep."

He sucked an unsteady breath into his lungs. "Get back up on the bed," he said, but he was disappointed when rather than a stern command, the words came out more like a plea.

She merely laughed. "I will if you will."

With a huff, he stretched out next to her, figuring the floor was probably so uncomfortable it would ward off any licentious thoughts he might have. But this close, he could smell her soft scent, part citrus shampoo, part warm woman.

"I never realized what a mean woman you are," he said after a couple of minutes.

"Thank you. I'm working on my mean side. Exercising it on a daily basis. I read a book recently, *Be a Bully*, that says to be truly happy, you have to do what you think is right, even if it upsets other people."

"Well, you'll be happy to know you're upsetting the hell out of me right now."

"Sorry about that," she said, but he didn't believe for a second that she meant her apology.

Long minutes ticked by while the two of them lay on the floor, side by side with only a ribbon of space separating their bodies. Chase tried to keep his mind on anything but the woman next to him. In his mind, he balanced the ranch's books, decided how much feed he needed to order when they got back to town, figured out what livestock he was going to enter in the state fair next year...

And wondered what color bra Megan had on. Maybe white, with lace. Or a pale pink, like her T-shirt.

Or maybe midnight-black. One of those that pushed everything up.

Chase groaned and jumped to his feet.

"Okay. You win." He grabbed his pillow and blanket

off the floor and tossed them on the mattress. Then he turned on the lamp, sprawled on the bed, and told her, "I give up. I've been trying to be a decent guy, but for the past couple of months, I've been shanghaied, bamboozled, and railroaded by everyone I know. I can't take it anymore. You want to have sex. Fine. Here I am. Have sex."

When Megan didn't say anything, he turned his head and looked at her. She stood next to the bed, her green eyes wide. He watched her debate her next action and felt the blood hum in his veins while he waited for her decision.

"Um, this isn't quite what I had in mind," she said. "I wanted it to be romantic."

"But sex isn't romantic," he pointed out, his emotions on a roller-coaster ride. He wanted her.

Really, really wanted her. But he also knew she'd end up getting hurt. "Sex is just sex, Megan. But hey, if that's what you want, then I'm willing to be a good friend and help you out."

She frowned. "Gee, thanks for the offer, but this isn't right, Chase. I'd feel like I was taking advantage of you," she said, although he noticed she put her pillow and blanket back on the bed. When she sat on the side of the mattress, he moved over to make room for her. "I can't have sex with you if you don't want to have sex with me."

"I'll survive." His heart raced in his chest, and he honestly didn't know what he wanted her to do. He couldn't stand this anymore, so he was trying to prove a point. He could only be pushed so far before he'd snap. But now, looking at her, he couldn't help wishing she'd take him up on his offer. "I thought this was what you wanted."

She shook her head. "Not like this," she said softly, and he figured she was talking more to herself than to him.

Without saying anything else, she reached out and turned off the light. Then she moved over to the far left side of the bed and said, "Good night, Chase." After a few minutes, he heard her breathing become soft and rhythmic. He figured it would be hours before he could fall asleep, but the bed really was comfortable, and he was exhausted. Not ten minutes later, he felt himself drifting off.

Right before he fell asleep two things crossed his mind—first, that Megan had managed to find a way to get him to share the bed with her after all.

And second, that he still couldn't help wondering what color bra she had on**

Megan tapped on the bathroom door. "Chase, are you all right? Has the swelling gone down yet?"

For at least a full minute there was no response. Then Chase threw open the bathroom door and frowned at her. "What did you say?"

He looked so yummy, standing there with only a towel wrapped around his waist, that Megan completely forgot what she'd said to him. Instead, she was one hundred percent focused on his tanned chest.

"Up here, Megan," Chase said dryly. "My face is up here."

"Hmm?" Blinking, she pulled her attention away from his chest and forced it to stay on his face. He must have just finished shaving because a tiny spec of shaving cream rested in the slight indentation in his chin.

"Megan," he said impatiently. "Pay attention."

She blinked again. A couple of times. Then tapped down on her libido and concentrated on what she'd been saying.

"I asked if the swelling has gone down yet," she said, not really surprised when her voice came out sounding more than a little breathless.

Again, he frowned at her. "I'm going to guess you're talking about the wasp bites and not something else. So yes, the wasp bites are better."

"Good." She glanced over his torso again, this time telling herself she was only looking at all that tanned, gorgeous skin to see if he was okay. One large purple bruise darkened his left side. "And the bruises? Do they still hurt?"

Chase sighed. "I'm fine. Let me finish getting dressed, then we can talk."

She looked back up at his face. "And the bump on your head? Is that fine, too?"

"Yeah. I'm in dandy shape."

With that, he closed the bathroom door again. Megan walked over and sat on the edge of the bed. Poor Chase. He was having a terrible day. It seemed the more things went right for her, the more they went wrong for him.

This morning she'd blissfully woken up in his arms. As much as she'd promised to stay on her side of the bed, she'd accidentally wandered over his way and wrapped herself around him like a vine.

For several wonderful moments, she'd simply

enjoyed being held by him. That was until he'd woken up, taken one look at her snuggled in his arms, and then jumped out of bed as if he'd caught on fire. Unfortunately, his foot snagged in the blanket, and he ended up crashing onto the floor, giving himself a couple of good-size bruises.

Then at breakfast, she'd had a wonderful time because Chase had been his most charming. He'd told her he wanted the trip to be enjoyable for her, so he'd decided to stop being a grouch. He'd made good on his promise by telling her funny stories. At least he had until a distracted waitress had whacked him, rather hard, in the back of the head with a metal coffee carafe.

Finally, once Chase had been feeling better, they'd headed over to the Alamo. Exploring had been fun and educational, and several times during their tour, she'd caught Chase looking at her with a lot more than mere friendship in his eyes. One of those times, when his gaze had locked with hers, she'd winked at him. The gesture must have startled him, because he'd backed into a tree and ended up getting stung by a couple of angry wasps.

But the absolute low point had come during their walk back to the hotel. A young man had hurried by them, bumping into Megan. When she'd started to lose her balance, Chase had grabbed her. Thanks to his quick thinking, she hadn't fallen in the water fountain they'd been walking by.

Unfortunately, Chase had.

Altogether, the poor man had had quite a day. Well, at least she had good news for him now.

The door to the bathroom opened, and Chase came

out. Although he looked wonderful, Megan couldn't help regretting that an unbuttoned cotton shirt covered most of his gorgeous chest and jeans covered his sexy legs.

"You look better," she said brightly.

He nodded. "Hard not to look better since earlier I looked like a drowned rat."

Not exactly a rat, but he had taken quite a dunking.

Hoping to make him feel better, she held up a room key. "I convinced Judy to let me rent another room, so we won't have to share tonight. You can sleep in this bed all by yourself without worrying about me taking advantage of you."

He stared at the key for a moment. "Judy must have wondered why you wanted another room. I mean, she thinks we're a happily engaged couple."

"She was curious, so I told her that you and I never spend more than one night together."

His blue eyes studied her intently. "Run that one by me again."

Megan shrugged. "I tried every other explanation I could think of, and she didn't buy a single one."

"No?"

Ticking them off on her fingers, she said, "I told her you needed time alone after the bad day you'd had, and she said I should be supportive and nurturing."

"That was sweet."

"Then I told her that you were mad at me, and she said you seemed like a really nice guy and you'd cool down eventually."

"I am thawing..."

"Finally, I told her I was mad at you, but she said all

I needed to do was tell you why I was upset, and she knew you'd do whatever it took to make the situation right."

"Intriguing."

Megan took a deep breath, then added, "At that point I had no idea what else to say so I told her we were superstitious and didn't want to spend more than one night together before the wedding."

Chase chuckled. "She must think we're odder than two alligators trying to ice skate."

"That's probably an understatement," she admitted, a smile tugging at her lips. "And I hate to think what she's going to tell Amanda. But I knew you'd be more comfortable if I moved to another room."

For several long seconds, Chase just looked at her, and Megan felt her heart race. *Say you want me to stay with you*, she chanted over and over in her mind.

Unfortunately, her telepathic abilities seemed to be on the fritz because what really came out of Chase's mouth was, "That'd probably be the best idea."

Drat. Oh well, it's not like she'd expected him to change his mind. That whack to the head he'd gotten hadn't been that hard.

Chase picked up his wallet and the room key. "I'll pay for the other room. And I'll be the one to move so you don't have to repack your things."

"Always the gentleman," she said, tracing the floral pattern on the bedspread with her index finger.

He sat down next to her. "I'm trying to be one, Megan. But like I said last night, I'm starting to run out of willpower."

As much as she hated herself for being thrilled to

hear him admit that, she was. Thrilled beyond words. Losing his willpower implied that he found it difficult to resist her, which in turn meant he felt a lot more for her than mere friendship.

There was hope yet.

"Why don't we discuss this over dinner?" she asked, standing and heading for the door. "After the day you've had, you must be hungry."

He smiled. "Sure. Let me finish getting ready." He stood and buttoned his shirt. Megan watched him dress, enjoying the feeling of intimacy caused by such an innocent action. Somehow watching Chase buttoning his shirt and tucking his wallet into his back pocket seemed very personal. This morning, he'd left the room while she'd gotten dressed, so she'd left the room when it had been his turn.

But watching him was exciting.

When he was done, he asked, "Ready?"

Mutely, she nodded and picked up her purse.

He must have misunderstood her silence, because he said, "You know, I've had a lot worse days on the ranch, so stop worrying about a few bumps." He grinned and added, "But for your own safety, you might want to give me a wide berth."

That was the last thing she wanted to do. What she really wanted was for Chase to kiss her senseless. Unfortunately, she knew that wasn't going to happen.

"Let's go," she said.

As they headed down the stairs, Chase asked, "Where do you want to eat?"

"Let's not tempt fate. Let's eat someplace away from the River Walk."

They asked Judy, who recommended a small barbecue restaurant just down the street from the B&B. Megan was worried that it would be a dark, intimate place, but instead it was rowdy and bright, with singing waitresses and food out of this world.

"This is a fun place," Chase observed, settling back in his chair.

Megan took a bite of her steak and felt as if she'd tasted heaven. "The food is wonderful."

When their waitress, Darla, stopped by again, she had a broad grin on her face and a couple of her coworkers in tow. "Judy from the B&B called. I understand you two just got engaged."

Oh, no. Megan subtly shook her head at Chase, but he seemed resigned to their fate.

"Something like that," he said.

Megan sensed what was coming and wanted to slip under the table, but no such luck. With a nudge to Chase, Darla said, "Well in that case, sweetie, you need to remember a few things if you're going to make a good husband."

With that, she and her two coworkers launched into the country song, "Any Man of Mine." As they detailed the many things Chase would need to do and say to make the woman in his life happy, Megan couldn't help smiling. The poor, poor man.

What else could life do to him today? The entire restaurant was watching him and laughing.

Thankfully, he took it well. He leaned back in his chair and nodded his head, as if he were trying to remember every warning the song gave. After Darla and company finished, he gave them a big tip and laughed.

"I guess that's better than getting hit in the head with a coffeepot," he said to Megan.

When he grinned at her, Megan smiled back. He was so wonderful. Not just his handsome-devil looks, but his humor and kindness. How could she not be in love with him?

She took a sip of her lemonade, her gaze locking on the assortment of fruit sitting in a bowl in the middle of the table. In the center was a pile of cherries—complete with stems. She'd ordered the fruit because she loved fruit—but now a variety of possibilities popped into her mind.

"I guess we head back to Honey in the morning," she said, still looking at the cherries.

"I guess."

"Did you enjoy this trip at all?" She held her breath, waiting for his response, more than a little bit afraid he'd say he'd had a terrible time.

"Yeah. I enjoyed it." His gaze was intent, heated. Megan's heart beat furiously in her chest. She loved the way he was looking at her, with fire and want and lots of good old lust in his gaze. Leaning forward, he added, "I always enjoy being with you."

Megan tucked that comment close to her heart. Then she gathered her nerve and plucked a cherry out of the bowl.

"Watch this," she said, holding Chase's gaze.

It took her a little bit of effort since she hadn't practiced nearly as much as she should have, but eventually, she managed to tie the cherry stem into a knot using only her tongue. She held out her handiwork for Chase to see.

"Ta-da," she said with a grin.

Chase looked as if he'd been struck by lightning. He made a mumbled, groaning sound as he first studied the knotted cherry stem, then glanced at her mouth.

"Party trick," she said softly.

"Come on." He stood and tossed money on the table. Then he wrapped his hand around hers, tugged her out of the restaurant, and hustled her back to the hotel. It wasn't easy keeping up with him, but she managed.

When they reached the bridal suite, she waited while he unlocked the door, dreading what would happen next. One of them was going to pack up their things and move to a room down the hall.

"Give me a moment to pack," she said, once they were inside the room.

As Chase tossed the key onto the dresser, Megan moved by him to get her suitcase. When she started to unzip it, he placed one hand on her wrist, stopping her.

"Hold on a moment."

His deep voice was husky, strained, and Megan moved closer to him. "Why?"

With a gentle touch, he brushed a strand of hair off her forehead. "You remember I mentioned earlier that my willpower was draining away?"

She couldn't believe what was happening here, or at least, what she hoped was happening here. Trying to contain her excitement, she kept her voice even when she said, "Yes."

He seemed almost as if he were looking into her soul. "I'm afraid I'm on dead empty, Megan." Then he bent his head and kissed her.

❧ 11 ❧

Megan didn't give him the chance to change his mind. As soon as he moved to kiss her, she rose up on her tiptoes and kissed him first. She threw herself at him with such gusto that he had to wrap his arms around her to keep them both from falling over.

"Whoa, whoa," he tore his mouth away from hers. "Sweetheart, let's not crash through the wall."

Megan kept kissing him. His cheek, his neck, his chin. "Kiss me," she murmured.

Oh, he intended on kissing her all right. He intended on doing a lot more than merely kissing her. But he also didn't want to end up in the hospital. Not now. Not when he'd finally decided to give in to the desire he felt for Megan.

He gave her another long, lingering kiss. Megan returned it with an enthusiasm that rocked him straight down to his boots. At the back of his mind, he still had a lot of reservations about making love with Megan. But he was only human, and he hadn't been kidding, his willpower had dried up quicker than rainwater in the Texas sun.

This time, one kiss led to another, then another. He couldn't seem to get enough of her. Although his hormones screamed yes, yes, reality smacked him in the face.

"Whoa."

She groaned and laid her head against his chest. "Stop saying whoa. Say giddy-up."

He chuckled. "I'll work on that. I only stopped this time because we've got a problem. I don't have anything with me."

She tipped her head back and looked at him. "By anything, do you mean like handcuffs or feathered boas?"

"No, I don't think we're going to need any help having a good time." Slipping his arms around her, he pressed his body against hers, enjoying the feel of her soft curves. "I meant I don't have any condoms with me, and I can hardly call downstairs and ask Judy to send up a few."

Rather than looking disappointed, a grin lit Megan's face. "I have the situation covered—literally." She walked across the room and picked up her cosmetic case and opened it. She removed the tray containing her makeup, then pointed inside. "Will these do?"

Chase looked inside. There were half a dozen boxes of condoms in all styles and colors.

"What in the world? Megan, you must have fifty condoms in here. Expecting reinforcements?"

She giggled and nudged him. "No. I just wanted to

be certain I got the right kind, and Mary said—" That stopped him cold. Mary Monroe was the wife of Ted Monroe, the owner of the one drugstore in Honey. "You bought all these condoms at Monroe's Drug Store?"

"Of course. At first, I felt a little embarrassed, but I knew they wouldn't mind answering any questions I had. If I'd gone to a big store in a different town, they might not have been as helpful."

Megan was looking at him as if there wasn't anything unusual about buying condoms from the biggest gossip in a town that thrived on gossip. He looked at the boxes in the bottom of her makeup case. At least Mary would tell everyone he had a lot of stamina.

"So Mary told you to buy all of these?" he asked, picking up one of the boxes.

"Oh, no. She recommended the ones with the car on the front, but Lilah said—"

Chase groaned. "Lilah Pearson was there, too?"

"Well, yes. She thought the ones with the sunset would be better. And then Troy Everson said the ones with the arrow on the front were really good."

With effort, Chase tried to pull air into his lungs. Finally, he managed, "Exactly how many people did you talk to about condoms?"

She shrugged. "Not that many. Four. Maybe five. And I didn't ask anyone's opinion. They noticed me looking and came over and made suggestions."

She squinched her eyes and admitted, "I guess I'd better tell you now that Nathan and Trent came into the store while I was there." She rooted through the boxes, finally pulling out one with a picture of a shooting star on the front cover. "They told me to buy these."

Chase took the box his brothers had recommended and tossed it into the trash. "No offense, but considering everything that's happened, I don't think I'll trust my brothers."

With that, he snagged one of the other boxes and tossed it on the bed. Then he nibbled on Megan's neck. "The whole town thinks we're here having wild sex, and yet, we're standing around talking."

She leaned toward him. "That does seem like a shame."

Leaning back, he held her gaze. "Megan, you know I won't change my feelings about love and marriage, right? You know that after this trip, I'm going to want to go back to being simply friends. Do you think you can do that?"

"I'll always be your friend, Chase," she assured him. "Tonight won't change anything. I promise."

◌⁜◌

THINGS HAD DEFINITELY CHANGED. MEGAN STOOD ON her front porch, debating what to say to Chase. The drive back from San Antonio had been fairly silent, but not uncomfortable. They both seemed to be caught up in their emotions from last night. Just thinking about how wonderful it had been to make love with Chase brought a silly grin to her face.

But last night had been last night, and now it was time to pay the piper.

"Thanks again for everything," she said as Chase

carried her suitcase into her house and set it on the living room floor.

"Since I'm not exactly sure what you're thanking me for, I'm not going to say 'you're welcome.'" He turned to face her. "Besides, I didn't do anything that deserves your gratitude."

Okey dokey. That sounded like a man who had picked up a few regrets on his trip to San Antonio. As usual, Chase was being hard on himself. As the oldest in his family—who'd practically raised his siblings—he held himself to impossible standards and never cut himself any slack.

Determined to keep things light, she said, "Fine, cowboy, have it your way. I had a great time."

He raised one dark eyebrow. "How do you mean that?"

Megan had to stop and think what she'd said, then she laughed. "I meant I'm glad you came with me on the trip, but you can take it the other way, too." Her bluntness seemed to throw him for a moment. He shifted his weight, glanced around her living room, then cleared his throat. "Guess it's about time we talk about what happened."

Even though she was far from psychic, she knew what he was going to say next. He intended on apologizing, which was the last thing she wanted to hear. So to prevent him from saying he was sorry the best night of her life had happened, she said, "I love you."

That certainly shut him up. For a second, at least. Then he sighed.

Uh-oh. A sigh wasn't a good sign. Not at all. Again, she hurried to prevent him from apologizing.

"Before you say last night was a huge mistake, I want to tell you something. I meant what I said. I love you. I've loved you for years as much more than a friend. And I think we can be happy together. But I also know you don't feel that way, and I accept that. I still want to be your friend. So, let's forget about last night and get back to being just friends."

"Megan, last night was just lust. Nuclear lust, I admit, but only lust. You can't let it convince you that you love me," he said softly.

She studied him for a moment, then said, "You know, sometimes you're one dumb cowboy."

That caught his attention. "Excuse me?"

"I mean it. If you think for one second last night was about lust, then you're acting dumber than mud." She'd never been more certain of anything in her life.

One corner of his mouth lifted, and she could tell he was fighting back a smile. "For a lady who claims to be in love with me, you sure are calling me dumb a lot."

"Oh, I love you. I feel bad that you're avoiding happiness like it's a giant pothole, but I still love you," she said, smiling despite her best intentions.

He finally let his smile break free and gathered her close for a hug. "You don't hate me?"

His question tugged at her heart. "No. I could never hate you."

He rested his chin on top of her head and rocked them slowly. "Because you know, what you're feeling is infatuation. It will fade, trust me."

With a groan, she shoved out of his arms. "There you go, being dumb again. Of course it isn't infatuation, and of course my feelings for you won't change. Give me some credit here, cowboy. I know love when I'm standing in it."

"I just meant—"

Megan held up one hand. "I know. Well, here's the deal. Since you're so convinced what we shared is only lust, then last night should have slaked our appetite for each other. I mean we did about everything a couple can legally do in Texas."

With a chuckle, Chase said, "I'm not too sure about that last little idea you had. I can't believe you read about that in a book."

"Books open new horizons," she said in her best librarian tone. "You can learn a lot from reading."

"Yeah, well, it certainly taught me a thing or two."

For a moment, they simply looked at each other, the memory of the previous night fresh and vivid between them. Then Chase broke eye contact.

Megan cleared her throat and forced herself to say the words she'd so carefully thought out during the ride home from San Antonio. "Anyway, now that we've made love, your sexual interest in me should wane since you don't love me."

He glanced back at her, the heat in his gaze still very real. But his response belied the look he was giving her. "Guess so."

"And in a few days, I'm sure we can go back to acting normal around each other." With effort, Megan pasted a bright smile on her face. What she was about to do was a calculated risk, but one she had to take. "Let's avoid each other for a while and let things cool down. I know, the playground committee is set to meet a week from

Tuesday. We can see each other then. We'll also use that as an opportunity to tell everyone we've called off our engagement."

For a moment, she thought Chase was going to argue with her, and she couldn't help hoping he would. She wanted him to say he couldn't stand the thought of not seeing her for eight whole days. But he didn't raise a single objection. Instead, he nodded his head.

He really was one dumb cowboy.

"Seems like the best idea." He shifted over to the front door. "Guess I'll see you at the meeting, then. And Megan, I know you're going to find any feelings you have for me will fade with time."

She sighed, but she might as well argue with his horse. Even after making love, Chase hadn't changed his mind about them.

After he drove away, Megan looked out her front window, surprised she didn't feel heartbroken. After all, Chase still maintained he didn't return her feelings. But rather than feeling heartbroken, she felt filled with expectation, like something wonderful was going to happen to her very soon. No doubt the sensation came from knowing that Chase loved her, too. Oh sure, he didn't want to love her. And he was going to fight it all the way. But she knew in her soul that he loved her.

From now on, she wasn't going to push him anymore. She'd done what she promised herself she'd do —she'd shown Chase how wonderful things could be between them. He needed to take the final step himself. He needed to decide if he wanted her in his life or not.

Smiling, she headed toward her bedroom to unpack.

She had every confidence that sooner or later, things would work out. One way or the other.

"But if he does decide he loves me and wants to build a life together," she muttered to herself. "I only hope our children get his looks and my common sense."

❧

"What do you mean you don't want to talk about it?" Leigh crossed the family room and flopped onto the couch near Chase. "You have to talk about the trip. I've been dying to hear what happened."

"I'm not telling you a thing." He picked up his beer and took a long sip. Then he nailed his sister with a narrow-eyed look. "And by the way, you're grounded until you're eighty-six for that little stunt with the hotel rooms."

Rather than even attempting to appear innocent, Leigh grinned. "Liked that, did you? So, what did you do? Sleep on the floor like a gentleman?"

"I already told you, I'm not saying a thing." When Leigh finally realized he really wasn't going to give her any details, she threw her hands in the air and bolted from the couch. "I'm going to call Megan."

"She won't tell you anything, either," Chase warned.

Leigh stared at him, her expression mutinous. "You can't do this. You owe it to the town to tell them what happened."

"You people need to get your own lives," he pointed out.

"I'm trying to, but since I'm grounded until I'm

eighty-six, it may be a little difficult." She headed toward the kitchen, turning when she reached the doorway. "By the way, I'm too old to be grounded by you. It's a useless gesture."

"Fine, then I'll have Trent arrest you instead," Chase said.

Leigh snorted. "You wish. I'm calling Megan."

After his sister flounced out of the room, Chase exhaled an exasperated breath. Women. They were driving him nuts. His original theory about the water still held true. The females in this town were acting weird.

Especially Megan. Why did she have to go and say she loved him? That's what he'd feared when he'd given into the lust he'd felt last night and made love with her. But he couldn't help himself. He'd never lost control like he had with her, but dang it, when she'd tied that cherry stem, he'd almost had a heart attack.

He really was one dumb cowboy. He sure had been last night, probably because all the blood had rushed from his brain to other organs, leaving him with limited common sense.

"Hey, if it isn't one half of the town's most famous engaged couple," Nathan said, wandering into the family room.

Chase studied his brother. "How'd you get in here?"

"Came through the front door. I haven't quite mastered walking through walls yet. But I'm working on it."

"Very cute." Chase took another big swig of his beer. Although he rarely drank, he figured even a teetotaler would need a drink after the weekend he'd had. Heck, the way his life was going, the devil himself would be nervous. "I thought I'd locked the front door to keep undesirable people—like you—out."

Nathan sat in the chair facing him. "Leigh was leaving and let me in. She said she was going to go see Megan and uncover the juicy bits about your trip."

"Juicy bits? What if there weren't any juicy bits? Did you people ever consider that?"

Nathan pretended to think for a second, then said, "Nope. No one is going to believe nothing happened. Not after several of us witnessed Megan stocking up on condoms at Monroe's Drug Store."

Chase might not be the sharpest hook in the tackle box, but he knew bait when he smelled it. If he acknowledged he knew what Nathan was talking about, then his brother in turn would know he'd found out about condoms during the weekend.

He eyed his brother. "Megan bought condoms?"

Nathan chuckled. "You're good, but not good enough. I can tell from looking at you that you and Megan did a lot more than sightsee in San Antonio."

"Bull," Chase said.

"It's not bull. You've got that look about you." Grinning, Nathan stood. "But I'm going to take off now before you turn mean and decide to take out your frustration on me."

"If, like you say, I got lucky this weekend, then why would I be frustrated?" Chase figured he'd nailed Nathan's cage shut with that observation.

But Nathan only said, "You're frustrated because

you want to be with her again, but you're fighting yourself because you think you're doing the right thing. You think you're protecting Megan, when in fact, you're hurting both of you."

"What in the blazes are you talking about?"

Nathan only shook his head. "Some things a man has to figure out for himself."

Before Chase could question him any further, Nathan left.

Of all the lamebrained comments to make. There was nothing to figure out. He'd made a mistake giving in to his desire for Megan, but he wasn't going to make the situation worse by acting like some greenhorn just because they'd had great sex. He'd had great sex before in his life. Okay, maybe not nearly as great as what he'd shared with Megan last night, but close to it.

Sort of.

But it wasn't love, and the more people tried to convince him he was in love, the more he knew he wasn't. Love was an illusion, like a magician sawing a lady in half. It wasn't real, and if you were foolish enough to believe, well, sooner or later, you'd find yourself holding a big bag of disappointment.

What he'd told Megan was the truth—the lust they'd felt for each other last night would fade in time. They'd taken the edge off the sexual hunger all that picturing each other naked business had created. And now, in a day or two, or certainly within a week, they'd be back to being friends. Only friends. More than likely, they'd laugh about what had happened.

And then, at last, his life could go back to normal.

Close to it, anyway. Sure, it was going to take some doing to get the image of Megan naked unhooked from his brain. But he'd find a way to do it. He had to, for both their sakes.

❧ 12 ❧

"There are no details to tell, so stop asking me," Megan told Leigh. "Besides, he's your brother. You shouldn't ask about things like this."

Leigh sighed and dropped into the chair facing Megan's desk.

For two days, the young woman had hounded Megan, trying to find out what did or did not happen in San Antonio. But since Chase had obviously told Leigh nothing, Megan wasn't going to tell her anything, either.

"Look, I'm not looking for specifics, because he is my brother and that would be too gross for words. All I want to know is if you managed to...you know, tiptoe through each other's tulips. If you did, then I figure I have a good chance of you becoming my sister-in-law."

"Tiptoe through each other's tulips?" Megan shook her head. "Where do you get this stuff?"

"He's my brother. I can't get more specific than that

without gagging. But you know exactly what I mean. Did you paddle his canoe? Dunk his cookies?"

"Wrap his Christmas presents?" Megan suggested with a laugh.

"Exactly. Well, did you?"

All Megan said was, "I can guarantee you that your brother and I never discussed Christmas on our trip."

Leigh leaned back in her chair. "Oh, perfect. Now I don't know if you mean the real Christmas or if you mean you two really didn't...stir each other's batter."

Megan laughed again, glad to have the chance to do something other than miss Chase. Leigh certainly knew how to lighten the mood, and even though she wasn't going to tell the younger woman a thing, it felt good to laugh.

"What did Chase tell you?" Megan asked.

"Not a blasted thing. The man's as silent as a mime, which ticks me off. But he's also getting grouchier by the day, which gives me hope. And yesterday, I caught him looking at the toothpicks again, which I'm absolutely certain is a good sign."

Leigh leaned forward again. "I don't suppose you've given any thought to coming by the ranch soon with a couple of cans of whipped cream? You really need to give that some serious consideration."

"Not likely," Megan said, although she and Chase had done a lot of other things. But a promise was a promise, and she was going to honor the agreement they had. She was going to avoid seeing him until next week at the playground committee meeting. In the meantime, she'd simply have to settle for reliving in her mind what they'd shared.

"Ah, come on, Megan. Give it a try," Leigh pleaded.

"I'm not coming out to the ranch with whipped cream, so stop suggesting it." Megan picked up two books from her desk and stood. "Now if you'll excuse me, I'm reading to the toddlers this week, so shoo."

Leigh groaned and stood. "Jeez, you're as mean is Chase. And here I am, just trying to be nice and help you become my sister-in-law. You never even thanked me for arranging for you and Chase to share the room in San Antonio."

"I'm not going to thank you, Leigh, because that was a terrible thing you did," Megan said. "I've told you time and again, Chase and I have to work through our relationship ourselves without other people butting in. I can't force him to fall in love with me. He either does or he doesn't. If he doesn't, then I'll accept it."

As she said the words, Megan realized they were true. As much as she loved Chase, and as much as she wanted him to love her in return, maybe he'd never be able to admit to himself that he loved her.

And if that happened, she'd simply have to make new plans for her life. She wouldn't sit around dreaming that he'd one day change his mind. No, if Chase didn't tell her he loved her after the meeting next week, then Megan was going to move on.

"Love doesn't work that way," Leigh said. "You can't turn it off like a light switch."

"This from a woman who has never been in love," Megan pointed out.

Leigh shrugged. "You don't have to know how to swim to tell when another person is drowning."

Megan appreciated her friend's concern, but she

couldn't make Chase do something he didn't want to do. "We'll just have to wait and see what happens. Patience, Leigh. We both need patience."

"I'd rather be rolled in tar and turned into a speed bump," Leigh said with another of her trademark snorts.

Megan patted her on the arm, then went to read to the toddlers. Truthfully, patience wasn't her strongest virtue, either. But she'd simply have to dig around and find some. Because there was no way she was going to rush Chase on this. And next week, regardless of what happened, she'd live with his decision.

🐾

"I WANT TO THANK EVERYONE FOR COMING TO THE meeting tonight. The kids are going to be overjoyed by the new playground. Don't forget that the ground-breaking ceremony is two weeks from Saturday," Megan said.

From his position by the door, Chase watched several of the committee members jot down the date. He wouldn't forget it. Everything having to do with Megan stuck in his mind like a thorn these days.

He kept his gaze focused on her, although she avoided making eye contact with him all night. He knew she was waiting for him to announce to everyone that their engagement was off. The truth was, he wasn't willing to say that until he'd had a chance to talk to her.

Things in his life weren't back to normal. Not by a long shot. Over the past week, he'd expected his interest in Megan to wane. After all, the sexual pull between them should be satisfied.

But to his horror, his interest in her had become obsessive to the point where he'd been thinking about her constantly, wanting to see her and be with her again.

Now, he was finally in the same room with her. If only this meeting would end. After what felt like a couple of eternities rolled into one, the ladies of the committee wandered out the front door, most of them flashing him flirty smiles on their way by. He returned their smiles with a polite nod. Hey, for all they knew, he was an engaged man. Didn't that mean anything to anyone anymore?

"Hey there, Chase," Janet said, coming over to stand close enough to see his DNA. "Rumor has it that you and Megan may be about to split up. No one's seen you together since you got back from San Antonio." She flicked one of the buttons on his shirt with a long, red fingernail. "If that's true, you should stop by later, and I'll help you mend your broken heart."

Chase had seen vultures use more finesse. He took a step back from Janet, causing her hand to fall away. "Thanks for the offer, but I'm fine. Have a nice night."

With that, he shoved open Megan's front door and waited for Janet to leave. She narrowed her eyes but must have decided he wasn't kidding, because with a small shrug, she headed out. But as she passed him, she said, "You really must be in love if you're turning me down."

Her comment caught him off guard. Unsure how to respond, he didn't say anything at all. Instead, he turned his attention back to Megan.

The living room was empty except for the two of them. Chase closed the front door, then walked over to stand next to her. The blood hummed through his veins; his heart raced in his chest.

She was collecting the trash, but she stopped and glanced up at him. "Hi."

"Hi. Let me help."

As they gathered up the dirty dishes, he admitted, "I've missed you."

She gave him a sweet smile. "I've missed you, too."

Her comment shouldn't make him happy, but it did. "I've thought a lot about you."

"I've thought a lot about you, too."

"I think we should talk," he said.

"I think we should talk, too."

He groaned. "Megan, if you keep echoing me, I'm going to start reciting dirty limericks."

With a laugh, she carefully placed the dirty cups back on the coffee table, then sat on the sofa. "In that case, I promise to stop echoing you, because I'm sure a cowboy like you knows some really dirty limericks."

"One or two," he agreed, sitting next to her. Now that he had her attention, he proceeded with caution, feeling like a jittery man in a nitroglycerin factory.

"I know you mentioned that after tonight we'd tell everyone we'd called off the engagement, but I was wondering what you thought about waiting for a while."

Her startled gaze met his. "Why?"

He saw no reason not to level with her. "Because I'd like to continue our relationship for a little bit longer."

"By relationship, do you mean our friendship?"

He held her gaze. He could tell she was confused.

Heck, he was confused too. "I mean our more recent relationship."

She frowned, obviously puzzled for a minute, then she said, "Oh, I see. You want to keep having sex."

When she put it that way, it sounded tacky. Yeah, well, maybe it was tacky for him to suggest. But he couldn't stop thinking about the night they'd shared. Couldn't help wanting it to happen again even though he knew it wasn't fair to ask.

"So rather than friends, we'll be lovers?"

"No, we'll be friends, too," he said firmly. "Just a little more than friends."

"Friends who have sex."

"Really great sex." A dopey grin crossed his face just thinking about it, but when Megan shot him a dry look, he wiped away the smile. This idea had made sense to him when he'd thought it over this morning, but now, seeing her reaction, he wasn't so sure.

"Do you love me?" she asked.

Chase had expected this question, and he wasn't going to lie to her. "You mean more to me than any woman I've ever met, which is why I want you in my life."

Megan's gaze held his as she asked, "Think you'll ever feel anything deeper for me?"

He had to be honest. "I don't believe in love. You know that. But I do believe that what we have is good. Hell, it's spectacular. I think we should appreciate what we have."

She closed her eyes, and for a second, he was afraid she was going to cry. But when she opened her eyes and looked at him, there wasn't a tear in sight.

"As tempting as your offer is, I'm going to have to pass. I realize it took a lot for you to admit you care for me, but you're never going to love me the way I love you. Chase, I'm just not willing to settle for second best."

"You're the most important person in my life. You'd never be second best," he told her.

"Yes, I would. And I deserve better." She stood and headed toward the door. "We want different things from life, Chase. I'm sorry, but it's best if you leave."

Chase scrubbed his face with his hands. He'd be hard-pressed to think of a way tonight could have gone any worse. Damn, this was exactly what he'd been afraid of all along. His friendship with Megan had been destroyed because he'd let the boundaries in their relationship blur.

"I wish I could tell you this would work out. I wish I could give you the pretty words and the promises, but I can't lie about this. Especially not to you," he admitted, knowing he was breaking her heart. His own heart felt more than a little squashed at the moment.

He reached toward her, wanting to offer her comfort. Wanting to soothe the injury as much as possible. But when he was close to Megan, he realized she didn't appear heartbroken in the least. In fact, she seemed remarkably calm. Resigned. He studied her face closely, looking for signs that she was putting on an act, but she seemed fine with what he was saying.

"Megan, I know you're upset about this, but—"

She shook her head. "I'm fine. You know, I read a book last week called *Build Your Own Sandcastle—Don't Live in His*. And it said that I shouldn't hang my dreams on those of a man. That book is right. I want a man who will love me to distraction. That man isn't you, so I'll simply have to keep looking."

Chase frowned. "Keep looking?"

"Yes. Just because you didn't fall in love with me doesn't mean the next man won't."

She opened her front door. "It shouldn't be too difficult to grab another man's attention. I learned a lot while I was trying to get you to notice me."

His blood ran cold. "You wouldn't."

"Why not?"

For one stupid second, he almost said she was engaged, but he caught himself in time. "You're not that type."

Her smile was wicked. "I am now. Thanks to you."

❧ 13 ❧

"**W**hat's wrong with you? If you get any meaner, you'll scare the bull," Trent said, tossing the basketball to Chase with enough force to almost knock the air out of his lungs.

"Nothing's wrong with me. I'm fine," Chase finally managed to say, although it was a lie.

He was miserable. Not seeing Megan was killing him. But there was no sense telling his brothers that, so he headed toward the basket. Since his mind wasn't on the game, Nathan easily got the ball away from him.

Nathan made a basket, then turned to look at Chase. "Not only are you mean, you're not paying attention."

"I have things on my mind," Chase said.

Trent looked at Nathan, then they both looked at him.

"Megan," his brothers said in unison.

Chase grabbed the ball away from Nathan. He hated

to think his brothers were right, but he knew they were. He'd spent the longest week of his life missing Megan, and now he couldn't think straight. He was going crazy, wanting to see her, to be with her.

"I don't want to talk about it," he said. "Let's play."

Nathan sat and leaned against the garage door. "No. I don't think so. You need to talk even if you don't think you do."

"Fine." Chase tossed the ball to Trent. "We'll play one-on-one."

Trent looked at Nathan, then at Chase, then back at Nathan. Finally, he wandered over and sat next to Nathan. "I figure I have a better chance of living to a ripe old age by siding with Nathan on this one. You need to talk about what's happening with Megan. You're like a big old dam. You'll burst if you don't reduce some stress."

Chase glared at his brothers. This was the problem with family. They pushed when you wanted to be left alone. The last thing he needed right now was grief from his brothers. He was already feeling like a horse had tossed him. He didn't want to fight.

"I told you. I'm fine," he said. To prove his point, he grabbed the ball and threw it. The ball soared, eventually hitting a tree nowhere near the hoop.

Nathan and Trent laughed. "Yeah, you seem just fine to me," Trent said. "But just in case, I think we should warn the birds."

Chase opened his mouth to argue, but he quickly realized there was no point. His brothers were right. He wasn't fine. Not at all.

He came over and sat on Trent's right. "Megan doesn't want to see me anymore."

Nathan leaned forward and looked at him. "She broke your engagement?"

"We were never engaged," Chase pointed out. "But we were...I mean we did become ...let's just say our relationship has changed recently."

Trent nudged Nathan, and they both grinned at Chase.

"I knew you two boogied in San Antonio," Trent said.

Chase ran his hands through his hair. Maybe asking his brothers for help was a bad idea.

"Never mind. I've got work to do." Chase stood.

"Settle down. Don't go storming off. Trent and I will behave," Nathan said, but only after giving Trent a sharp look. "Now tell us what the problem is."

"I don't think so. The last time we discussed my personal life while playing basketball, you two dimwits gave me advice that blew my nice, orderly life all to hell. You told me to flirt with Megan, that a kiss or two would prove to her that we had no chemistry."

"But you had so much chemistry that things went kaboom, right?" Trent asked.

Chase wasn't about to discuss his sex life. All he was willing to say was, "Sort of."

Rather than appearing contrite, his brothers grinned once again. Great. So much for finding a sympathetic ear around this place.

"You want to know what your problem is?" Nathan asked.

Chase glared at him. "No."

Without hesitating, Nathan said, "You never see what's standing directly in front of you. Megan has been in love with you for years, but you never saw it."

"We're friends. At least we were. I don't think we are anymore." Even saying the words hurt. Megan had been a great friend to him. He was going to miss her.

"You're a jackass," Trent said, standing and retrieving the ball. It went through the hoop with a whoosh. "Megan loves you. You love Megan. And if I'm understanding you right, the two of you howled at the moon in the bedroom. So that's that. Bing. Bang. Happy ending."

Nathan nodded. "Seems pretty easy to me as well."

"Megan wants love and forever. Let's face it. No one we know is happily married, and Megan already turned me down when I suggested we keep things casual."

Nathan stood and walked over to Chase. "Some-times love does last. I can think of a lot of couples who are still going strong after twenty, thirty years."

"Name one of those couples," Chase challenged.

Just as he expected, Nathan couldn't immediately list one.

"You can't think of one, can you?" Chance said.

Nathan shrugged. "Give me a moment."

Trent laughed. "I've got one. Conrad and Amanda Newman. They've been married forever."

Nathan nodded, his expression turning smug. "That's right. And the Monroes. They've been together a long time."

"And Earl and Fran. Married for years." Trent

bounced the ball as he said, "Guess you're wrong, buddy boy. Lots of couples last."

Although his gut instinct was to dismiss what his brothers were saying, Chase had to admit they were right. Those three couples had been together a long time and still were happy.

"I guess," he eventually conceded. "Maybe some people know the secret to making love last."

"I don't think there's a secret," Nathan said. "I think they work at it and don't take each other for granted."

"It's kind of like this ranch. You work hard to keep it going. I believe you'd work equally hard on keeping your marriage happy."

With effort, Chase swallowed past the lump in his throat. "Marriage? I'm not even sure I love her."

Trent shoved him. "Sure, you love her. That's why you miss her so much. And you should be thinking about marriage. You can't take a woman like Megan away for a wild weekend of crazy sex and not ask her to marry you." He shook his head. "Damn, Chase, I thought you knew better than that."

Indignation filled Chase, more on Megan's behalf than on his own. "I didn't say we had a wild weekend of crazy sex."

"Oh, give it up, Chase." This came from Leigh, who had walked out the kitchen door. "You're not fooling anyone. You and Megan made love. Everyone knows it. In fact, I was in Palmer's Grocery yesterday, and Betty Ann said she thought you and Megan had been fooling around for years."

"No, we haven't," Chase said.

"I don't think I believe you. I think Betty Ann may be right," Leigh countered.

"No, she's not. Megan and I never made love until —" He caught himself, but not in time. He was wasting his breath. "It doesn't matter."

"When you first made love doesn't matter," Nathan said, patting him on the arm. "But the fact that you're in love with Megan matters a great deal. You have to accept that you love her."

Trent bobbed his head. "Yep. It's either that, or you need to forget about her." His expression brightened. "Hey, if you're not interested in Megan, maybe I could—"

Chase silenced his brother with a glare. "Don't you dare say it. Not about Megan. If you try to make a move on her, I will tear you apart."

"Spoken like a man in love," Trent said.

Chase had to agree. As soon as the words had left his mouth, he'd realized their importance. The raging jealousy that filled him at his brother's teasing crystallized his feelings. He really did love Megan. Loved her more than anyone else he knew. Over the past few weeks, he'd seen both himself and Megan in a new light. He couldn't believe it had taken him so long to be ready to accept her as more than a friend.

He really was one dumb cowpoke.

But one fear still gnawed at him. "What if we can't make it work?" He scanned the faces of his brothers and his sister. "What if this doesn't last? I couldn't stand to see Megan hurt like that."

Nathan smiled and said with confidence, "You'll just

have to make certain your love does last. Shouldn't be a problem. Your friendship has lasted for years."

So many questions roared through Chase. Could his siblings be right? Could he make the love he felt for Megan last a lifetime?

Leigh sighed. "Chase, answer me this—are you willing to never see Megan again?"

"No," he said without hesitation. "I couldn't take that."

"Are you willing to stand around while she marries someone else?" Leigh asked.

"No," he said firmly. Just the thought of her marrying someone else made him crazy.

"Then that's your answer," Nathan said. "It's like the old saying goes, sometimes you don't know what you've got until you lose it. Well, you've lost Megan. What are you going to do about it?"

"I might already be too late," Chase said.

"She didn't fall out of love with you this quickly. Convince her you mean business," Leigh said.

"How?"

Trent grinned, then looked at Nathan and Leigh. "Stick with us. We'll figure something out. Devious ideas come naturally to the Barretts."

"THIS PLAYGROUND IS GOING TO BE GREAT," EARL Guthrie said as he came to stand next to Megan. "It's going to mean so much to the kids of Honey."

Megan looked around the park. Yes, the playground was going to be great. At least one of her dreams had come true. Too bad the other one hadn't worked out.

"I appreciate all of your help," Megan said.

Earl grinned. "I didn't do anything but help nudge your idea along. You did all of the convincing yourself." He glanced around. "Big crowd here today, but I haven't seen Chase. Where are you hiding him?"

The crowd for the groundbreaking ceremony was large. Very large. But she knew for a fact that Chase wasn't here. She'd looked repeatedly for him.

"He hasn't arrived yet," she said.

Earl rocked back on his heels and peered at Megan over the top of his glasses. "Everything okay?"

Now was the time to tell him that the engagement was off, but Megan couldn't seem to form the words. "Fine."

He continued to study her. "You sure about that? You seem a bit pale. You feeling okay? Not pregnant, are you?"

Megan almost swallowed her tongue. "No, of course I'm not pregnant."

"Calm down. Seemed like the logical conclusion, what with you and Chase being so in love." He pointed at the lone tree in the far corner of the park. "I remember what young love is like. I was so crazy about Fran that I carved our initials in that tree over there. Now we have five children and eleven grandchildren. Falling in love's the most natural thing in the world."

Not the way she'd been going about it. There was nothing natural about how she'd tried to force Chase to fall in love with her. But she'd learned all the books were wrong. You can't make someone love you.

Apparently sensing her unhappiness, Earl patted her shoulder. "He'll come around. He's a good man, so don't worry. It took a while for me to come to my senses, too. But in the end, things with Fran and me worked out. The same will happen with you and Chase. I know it."

Earl was being so kind, Megan felt obligated to be honest with him. "About our engagement—"

Earl winked. "I didn't just tumble out of the cabbage patch yesterday, you know? But like I said, things will work out."

With that cryptic statement, the mayor walked away. Megan watched him go, wishing she could believe him. Wishing there was even a glimmer of hope that things would work out with Chase.

But how in the world could they?

"I told you to try the whipped cream," Leigh said as she came over to stand by Megan. "You look miserable, but it's your own fault. If you'd tried my whipped cream idea, you'd probably be locked in some tacky motel room with Chase right now, doing things that would make a Kama Sutra scholar blush."

Megan felt the warmth of a blush climb her own cheeks. "Hello to you, too."

Leigh studied her face. "Seriously, are you okay? You look odd. Are you pregnant?"

Exasperated, Megan sighed. "Jeez, everyone in this town has a one-track mind. First Earl. Now you. No, I'm not pregnant. I'm just upset that Chase isn't here today."

Leigh shoved her sunglasses onto the top of her head. "That's what happens when you sleep with your friends. Things get confused."

"If memory serves me, you were all for me having a physical relationship with your brother."

Nodding, Leigh regarded her closely. "Oh, I was. I still am. I just think you didn't have enough of a physical relationship. You forgot the whipped cream. That would have cinched this deal."

Megan opened her mouth to argue with Leigh, but before she could say a word, the younger woman muttered something about being late and took off.

Left alone, Megan scanned the crowd, hoping against hope that Chase had decided to come to the ceremony. But there was no sign of him, so she sat in one of the folding chairs in the front row. She'd worked so hard to make this day happen, and now that it was here, she felt more than a little sad. She'd wanted Chase to share this moment with her. He should be here. Even though things had ended badly between them, he was the co-chair of the committee. He should be at the groundbreaking.

After a few minutes, Leigh came and sat next to Megan. "I guess the speeches will start soon." She made a snoring noise. "Keep yours short, okay? I have a date this afternoon."

"I'll try," Megan assured her. She pulled her index cards out of her pocket. "I don't have a lot to say except thank you."

After a couple of minutes, Earl started the ceremony. First, he recapped the history of the project and how much money the carnival and auction had made. Then he smiled at Megan.

"Now here to say a few words is the lady who made all this happen—Megan Kendall."

Megan walked over to the podium, stacked her index cards neatly, then looked out at the crowd.

And froze. Chase stood directly in her line of sight, a lopsided grin on his handsome face. Megan's heart raced, joy rushing through her. He'd come to the ceremony after all.

As she looked at him, she realized she'd been kidding herself. No way could she walk away from this man. She'd told him she didn't want to continue their relationship if there was no love on his side, but now, looking at him, she realized that was hooey. In his way, she knew Chase loved her. He might not call it the same thing, but she felt his caring in his touch and in the heated looks he gave her.

She could see his love right now in his smile. The man cared for her and would never intentionally hurt her. She was the one hurting herself. Hurting both of them.

Well, that was a mistake that could quickly be remedied. After the ceremony, she'd tell him she was willing to continue being lovers. Anything. As long as they were together.

Feeling like a cartoon anvil had been lifted off her head, she smiled back at Chase.

"Remember what I told you last time," Leigh said, not even attempting to keep her voice down. "If you're nervous during your talk, picture Chase naked."

Megan laughed, as did most of the people sitting near Leigh. Megan's gaze met Chase's, and his grin only grew. He knew what she was picturing in her mind.

"Megan, honey, why don't you go ahead and give your speech, then you and Chase can go someplace quiet and stare at each other all day long if you want. I need to get home in time for supper," Earl said.

Megan blinked and looked at her cards. That was love for you. She was standing in front of most of the town of Honey making puppy eyes at Chase.

As quickly as possible, she ran through her speech. Thank goodness for her index cards. Without them, she would have forgotten everything she planned on saying. But she did remember to thank everyone who had helped with the fundraiser. Finally, she looked at Chase. "Of course, a big thank you goes to Chase Barrett, for helping me when I needed him most. I couldn't have done it without you."

The crowd hollered and clapped loudly, and Earl stood, apparently ready to move on. But when Chase started walking toward the podium, silence fell over the crowd. Everyone swiveled their heads between Megan and Chase, watching the two of them closely.

"Mind if I say something?" Chase asked no one in particular. "I never made a secret of the fact that I wasn't keen on being on this committee. But I have to say, I'm glad I was. Not only so I could help the kids in this town get a sorely needed playground, but also because I learned a lot of things while helping out. I learned Earl never hears the word no, doesn't matter how loud you say it."

That comment brought a chuckle from the crowd. Chase continued walking toward Megan. "I learned that my brothers and sister might be a massive pain some of the time, but when it really counts and I need them, they stand by me."

Another chuckle rolled through the audience.

"Finally, I learned the most important thing I've ever learned. I learned Megan Kendall loves me." Megan sucked in a tight breath, waiting anxiously for what he would say next.

"And I learned I love her back."

Stunned, Megan stared at Chase. Had she really heard what she thought she'd heard? "What did you say?" she asked, her voice barely above a whisper.

But she could read the answer to her question on his face. Love lit his features and danced in his deep-blue eyes.

"I love you," he said, his gaze locked with hers. "I have for a long, long time."

Happiness filled Megan, and she smiled. "Me, too."

Chase smiled back at her. "Just so Megan and everyone in this town never forgets how I feel, my family and I made a little something for the park." Nathan and Trent appeared at the back of the crowd. With a lot of jostling and teasing, they slowly made their way forward. They carried a large object wrapped in a thick striped blanket. When they were directly in front of Megan, they set the object next to Chase.

"Megan, I didn't want to hurt that poor tree, but I wanted a way to show you and the entire town of Honey how I feel."

With that, Chase pulled away the blanket. Underneath was a handcrafted wooden bench. Megan had never seen anything so beautiful. The workmanship was amazing.

But what amazed her most was the message carved into the back of the bench. It read: Chase loves Megan.

She felt the warmth of tears trickle down her face,

but she couldn't seem to stop them. For so very long, she'd dreamt of having this wonderful, caring, sexy man return her love. Now he finally did.

She took a step toward him, but before she could reach his side, he went down on one knee. More than a few of the citizens of Honey were standing on their chairs to watch, but Megan didn't care. All she cared about was the man kneeling in front of her.

"Megan Kendall, will you marry me?" he asked.

Through her tears, Megan nodded, unable to get the words out. In her entire life, she'd never been at a loss for words, but she was now.

She rushed to Chase and tugged him back up to his feet. Then she wrapped her arms around his neck and kissed him. A loud "ah" came from the crowd, but Megan just kept kissing Chase.

"You really love me?" Megan asked when they finally stopped kissing long enough to catch their breath.

"Yes. I'm sorry it took me so long to come to my senses." He cupped her face in his hands. "I can't believe I almost lost you."

She smiled, knowing their life together was going to be filled with love and laughter and many, many happy years. "You never even came close to losing me. I'd already decided I wasn't giving up yet." She kissed him again soundly, then explained, "See I still had one last trick I hadn't tried yet."

"And what would that be?"

"It involves showing up at the ranch wearing racy underwear and carrying a couple of cans of whipped cream. I was assured that you'd fall in love with me long before both cans were empty."

Chase grinned. "I like that idea. A lot."

Megan was kissing Chase again when Earl pointed out they needed to wrap up the groundbreaking ceremony. And as she stood next to the man she loved, she used her shovel to break ground on the playground she knew her own children would one day use.

"Ready to go home?" Chase asked almost an hour later.

Megan anxiously nodded. Although she'd enjoyed the ceremony, she was dying to be alone with the man she loved.

"Want to come to my house or go to the ranch?" she asked.

"Let's go to your house. It's closer, and I'm anxious to get you alone." They were almost to the parking lot when he added, "But I need to make a stop on the way."

"Where?"

His smile was wicked and downright wonderful. "Palmer's Grocery. I thought we'd pick up some whipped cream." With a wink he added, "And maybe a few cherries."

❦

Dear Reader,

Readers are an author's life blood and the stories couldn't happen without **you**. Thank you so much for reading! If you enjoyed *Handsome Rancher,* we would so appreciate a review. You have no idea how much it means to us.

If you'd like to keep up with our latest releases, you

can sign up for Lori's newsletter @ https://loriwilde.com/sign-up/.

Please turn the page for an excerpt of the next book in the The Handsome Devil series, *Handsome Boss*.

To check out our other books, you can visit us on the web @ www.loriwilde.com.

EXCERPT: HANDSOME BOSS

Some men should never wear a shirt, Emma Montgomery decided as she watched Nathan Barrett shoot baskets on the sports court behind his house. The man was poetry in motion—a Shakespearian sonnet, a love poem by Keats.

He spun toward her and her gaze skittered down his muscled chest again. Or maybe a really naughty limerick.

Yep, he was a handsome devil alright.

"You wait here," Leigh Barrett said from the passenger seat of Emma's compact car. "I need to talk to Nathan for a second."

Now that didn't sound good. Not good at all. Emma pulled her gaze away from Nathan and looked at his sister.

"You assured me that everything was set," Emma pointed out Leigh bobbed her head, her short black hair brushing against her chin. "It is set, so stop worrying."

Not in the least reassured, Emma asked, "Nathan knows I'm coming, right?"

Again, the head bob. "You bet."

"And he agreed that I could have the technical writing job?"

"Yep, that, too."

Still unable to shake the feeling that she'd stepped off the side of a mountain and was about to take one heck of a plunge, Emma pressed on. "And he did agree that I could use his garage apartment this summer, right?"

"Everything is fine." Leigh shoved open the door to the car. "You're such a worrier, Emma. No wonder you live on antacids. You need to relax. Take a few deep breaths. Find your center."

"My what?"

"You know. The child within. Your feminine side." With a grin, she added, "Feng shui yourself."

Emma laughed and felt the tension level inside her slip down a notch or two. She should have known when push came to shove, Leigh wouldn't let her down. She knew how much Emma needed this summer job.

"I promise to relax if you're certain everything is fine."

Leigh rolled her eyes. "Say it slowly with me: 'Ev...er...y thi...ng is fi...ne.'"

Emma smiled. "Everything is fine."

Leigh glanced at her brother, then back at Emma. "Very good. Now give me a head start. I just need to clarify one tiny detail with Nathan, then we can get you moved into the garage apartment."

There was something in the way Leigh said the

words "one tiny detail" that made the feeling of dread rush right back into Emma's stomach and settle down for a long stay. Something was rotten in Denmark, or rather in Honey, Texas. This small town might call itself the "sweetest town in Texas," but right now, she had the distinct feeling that everything wasn't "sweet."

Emma didn't want to ask. Not at all. Intuitively she knew she wasn't going to like the answer. But she had to know, so squinting in an attempt to lessen the expected blow, she asked, "What detail do you need to clarify with Nathan?"

"Oh, nothing special," Leigh said. "I just need to mention a few things." She swung her legs out of the car, then said in a rush, "Like that you're going to work for him at his software company for a few weeks while you live in the apartment over his garage. No biggee."

Emma's mouth dropped open, but before she could say a word, Leigh sprinted away from the car. No biggee? This was a really big biggee. Nathan Barrett knew absolutely nothing about her plans.

Good grief. Fumbling in her purse, Emma tugged out her roll of antacids and tossed a couple into her mouth. The familiar chalky taste brought her a tiny degree of comfort.

"You can do this," she muttered, willing the butter-flies—no make that condors--thrashing around in her stomach to chill. "You can handle this."

Even though she only half believed herself, she climbed out of her car. Leigh was already on the basket-ball court, talking with her brother.

"Darn her," Emma muttered, slamming her car door. She should have known better than to trust her summer plans to Leigh Barrett. Leigh was funny and full of life and great to be around, but she was also kooky, and crazy, and often unreliable.

The last character trait was the one Emma should have focused on when Leigh had brought up this idea about coming to Honey. She should have checked and double-checked these plans like a bride planning a flawless wedding.But she hadn't questioned a thing.

"You coward," she muttered to herself as she reached the outer corner of the sports court.

She hadn't questioned Leigh simply because her friend had promised the solution to all her problems. Leigh had assured Emma that her brother needed a technical writer for a few weeks and that the pay would be great.

And when Emma had mentioned she'd need a place to stay, Leigh had had the answer to that one, too. Nathan had a nice apartment over his three-car garage.

What could be better? She'd be able to work on her dissertation in the evenings after she came home from Barrett Software. And she'd pick up some nice change to pay the never-ending college bills.

What a dummy. She might as well tattoo the word sap on her forehead. Just because she'd wanted this job to work out wasn't an excuse not to check her facts before leaving Austin and driving to Honey with Leigh. Her super-organized father would be appalled that she hadn't verified the plans.

At the moment, jobless and homeless, she was pretty appalled, too.

As she approached Leigh and her brother, she heard Leigh hastily explaining the situation while Nathan frowned. The man wasn't pleased. That much was obvious. He glanced in Emma's direction, then walked over and grabbed a T-shirt off a bench and pulled it on.

"It's no big deal," Leigh was saying as Emma drew even with them.

"It's a very big deal," Nathan shot back. He turned and looked at Emma. "Hello."

Wow. Nathan was even better looking close up. Every female hormone in Emma's body sat up and took notice, and for the briefest of moments, Emma forgot her jobless/homeless problem and simply enjoyed looking at him.

"Nathan, this is my friend, Emma Montgomery," Leigh said. "Emma, this is Nathan, who will help me out, or I'll tell all of his secrets."

Nathan glanced at his sister. "What secrets? I don't have any secrets."

Leigh snorted, an unladylike sound that oddly fit her personality. "Oh, please, sell it to someone who's never met you. I know all the good things. Like that you cried for an hour the first time a girl kissed you—"

Nathan frowned. "I was six."

"Or the time when you had a crush on Lindsey Franklin, so you kept calling her up, but when she'd answer, you'd hang up—"

"I was eleven."

Leigh put her hands on her hips and said, "Best of all, how about the time in high school when MaryLou Delacourte's parents thought she was at a slumber party when actually she was with you, and you two were—"

"Stop." Nathan tipped his head and looked at Emma, humor gleaming in his amazing blue eyes.

Despite being annoyed at his sister, there was a healthy dose of brotherly love obvious in his treatment of Leigh. He might not be happy with what she'd done, but he was being an exceptionally good sport about it. "Do you have any objections to being a material witness to a crime?"

Emma laughed. "Under the circumstances, I completely understand."

"Ha, ha. Like you'd ever do anything to me." Leigh leaned up and gave her brother a loud, smacking kiss on his cheek. "Jeez, you're sweaty."

"I was shooting hoops and not expecting company," he said. His gaze returned to Emma "Sorry."

"I'm the one who's sorry. I had no idea this wasn't arranged." She frowned at Leigh. "I was under the impression you knew all about the plans. I guess I should head on back to Austin."

"Nathan Eric Barrett, how rude can you be?' Leigh scolded. "Look what you did."

"What I did? I haven't done anything to anyone," he said calmly. "Go inside, Leigh. I want I talk to Emma alone."

"But if I'm not here——"

"Go inside," Nathan repeated.

Finally, muttering and fussing the whole way, Leigh headed across the sports court and disappeared inside the large, brick house.

Left alone with Nathan, Emma tried to keep her gaze firmly tacked on his face. Boy-oh-boy, it wasn't easy. His T-shirt hugged his muscles, but since she hated it when men talked to her chest, she imagined Nathan would hate it if she had a conversation with his pecs.

"So, if I'm following this, Leigh told you I had a job opening for a technical writer at Barrett Software," Nathan said.

Emma nodded, hoping against hope that at least a little bit of Leigh's story had been true. She crossed her fingers. "Do you?"

His expression was kind. "I'm sorry, no."

"Oh." She swallowed past the nervous lump in her throat and struggled to maintain control. Breathe, Emma. Breathe.

She fumbled in her pocket, searching for her antacids, then remembered they were in her purse. That was okay. She could handle this. Sure, there weren't a lot of really great jobs lying around that would only last the summer. And sure, she'd been counting on this job to help pay off some bills. But she could manage. She hadn't made it all the way to the doctoral program at the University of Texas without becoming a pro at dealing with problems. This was only a setback. A big setback, granted, but one she could handle.

"I see," she managed to say when Nathan continued to give her a sympathetic look.

"I understand that Leigh also promised you could live in the apartment above my garage." This time, it was a statement, not a question.

The feeling of dread she'd been experiencing now took on monumental proportions. "Let me guess, you don't have an apartment over your garage, either."

"Yes, I do."

She nodded. "Of course you—you do?" Blinking, she tried to decide what that meant. Could this possibly be a tiny streak of good luck struggling to shine through the dark cloud?

"Yes, but it's my storage room, filled with old junk. Not really suitable to live in at the moment" Ah, heck. Emma blew out an exasperated breath. Great. Just great No job. No place to live. Talk about with friends like Leigh, who needed enemies.

"Well, that's that. I guess I'd better go. Thank you for your time," she said.

Nathan grinned. "You give up too easily." He tossed her the basketball, which she just managed to catch. "Do you play?"

She looked at the ball in her hands. "What?"

"Sink it."

With a shrug, she turned, assessed her shot and neatly sunk the ball. When she turned back to look at Nathan, he nodded.

"Nice shot."

"I played in high school," she told him. "Look, why don't I say goodbye to Leigh and head back—"

"Wait" Nathan wandered over and picked up the basketball. He dribbled it as he came back over to stand next to her. She tried, really she did, to keep from staring at him, but how much was a woman supposed to resist? The man was gorgeous, absolutely gorgeous, and despite the disappointment flooding through her at the moment, she wasn't dead.

"Do you know why I sent Leigh inside?" he asked, a roguish gleam in his eyes.

Emma considered the possibilities, finally settling on the most obvious. "Because you were afraid you'd do something terrible to her if you didn't?"

He chuckled, the sound warm and rich and electrifying as it danced across Emma's skin. This man was like fudge ripple ice cream. Much, much too tempting.

"I sent Leigh inside so she could sweat for a little while. Even without looking, I know she's watching us through the kitchen window, wondering what we're talking about."

Emma glanced toward the house and caught a glimpse of Leigh peering through the window before she disappeared. "You're right. She's there."

Nathan smiled. "I know. See she's about ninety-nine percent sure I'll save her. I always have in the past. But there's that one percent of uncertainty, the tiniest fragment of doubt, that's making her climb the walls. I figure the least I can do is make her squirm for a few minutes before I save her."

Emma snagged onto what he'd said. He'd save Leigh? Did that mean she would get a job and a place to stay after all? Was it too soon to yell yahoo and dance around with joy?

She studied Nathan and tried not to let her optimism run away with her, but she couldn't help asking, "Are you saying you do have a job?"

"A couple. Neither of them is for a technical writer, though." His gaze skimmed her casual outfit of jean shorts and a green T-shirt, then nodded to-ward the basketball. "Want to try to make that shot again?"

At this point, Emma would do just about anything to get a job. She didn't have time to waste going back to Austin and seeing if she could scrounge up something at the university. "Sure."

He tossed her the ball, and she sunk it.

"You're good." For a second, he studied her, and Emma's pulse rate picked up. As much as she'd like to attribute the metabolic change to being nervous, she knew that was bunk. Her heart was racing because she was attracted to Nathan. Very attracted.

"Tell me about yourself," Nathan said.

This was hardly the place she would have picked for an interview, but at this point, she was willing to be interviewed in the middle of Interstate 20 if it meant she could get a job.

"I'm working on my doctorate in English at the University of Texas," she told him.

"That's where you met Leigh."

"Yes." She glanced toward the house, then added, "And up until a few minutes ago, we were great friends."

Nathan laughed again, and Emma had to admit, that was a sound she could get used to without any trouble. "It's not that bad. Things will work out. My brothers and I are used to doing damage control when necessary to pull Leigh out of the fire."

"That doesn't upset you?"

Nathan snagged the ball again and easily made a shot. "Don't get me wrong. I don't approve of Leigh's methods. But she's just that way. Always has been. It's part of her personality...part of her charm."

"Being devious and conniving?"

His grin was devilish. "Yes. You'll get used to it."

Emma sincerely doubted that. "Does that devious streak run in your family?"

Nathan's smile was oh-so enticing. "Me? I'm completely harmless."

Yeah, right, and she could wrestle crocodiles.

**

This time, Leigh had really taken the cake. Nathan glanced at the house and wondered not for the first time how pure mischief could flow through his sister's veins. Even for her, this was a bit much. Not only was she yanking him around, but she was also embroiling one of her friends in whatever this latest scheme was. A friend who was obviously upset.

He'd bet his new car that Leigh's motives were far from pure. If he had to guess, he'd bet his sister was up to something.

Leigh was always up to something.

And it didn't take a rocket scientist to figure out what. The data was pretty clear. Leigh had arranged for Emma Montgomery to not only spend the summer working at Barrett Software, but she'd also managed to have Emma living at his house. Emma, who just so happened to be smart and gorgeous--two traits he greatly admired in a woman, which Leigh knew. Could his sister be trying to fix him up? He knew she was tired of him interfering in her life. But tired enough that she'd go this far?

The concept was almost too diabolical to entertain. That would mean Leigh was willing to use her friend Emma as bait. Could Leigh actually be that sneaky?

He sighed. Of course she could. He knew for a fact that she'd meddled in their brother Chase's life, fixing him up with the town librarian. Sure, Chase and Megan made a great couple, but he didn't want to be fixed up, especially not by Leigh.

He glanced back at Emma. Did she realize she was a victim? Did she know her friend was setting her up? He wasn't picking up any flirtatious vibes from her, so he was fairly certain she truly was here simply for a job.

But when she smiled at him, Nathan felt his heart rate rev. She really was gorgeous.

"Think we should stretch this out a little longer and make Leigh squirm some more?" he asked.

Emma nodded. "Absolutely. Squirming is good for her."

Nathan couldn't help pointing out, "I see a little deviousness runs in your family, too."

"Apparently."

He looked at his house. Leigh stood at the kitchen window, watching them.

She was guilty all right.

He turned his attention back to Emma. She had wavy auburn hair that hung to her shoulders. Auburn hair was his personal favorite. Or rather, it had become his favorite in the past few minutes. Emma also had his favorite color eyes—hazel. Again, his propensity for hazel eyes was a recent discovery, but still, he really liked that shade. A lot

Eyes like Emma Montgomery's seemed to change color every few minutes. At the moment, they were a steely gray—sharp, intense, not missing a thing.

The back door to the house flew open and banged against the outside wall.

"I can't take it anymore, Nathan," Leigh hollered from the open door to the kitchen. "I swear if you send Emma home, you'll no longer be my favorite brother."

Nathan grinned and winked at Emma. "Is that a promise?"

"Ha, ha. Now stop tormenting us and help un-pack

Emma's car. You two have to go to work tomorrow. You can't stand around here all day yammering on the basketball court." Without waiting for his response, Leigh headed over to the small yellow compact car parked in his driveway.

"Guess she told us," Nathan said, waiting for Emma to precede him to her car.

"You know, we don't have to do what she says," Emma pointed out. "I mean, you don't have to give me a job...if you really don't want to."

Nathan knew that. Just because Leigh might have concocted some sort of scheme didn't mean he was going to fall for it. Oh sure, he'd let Emma work at Barrett Software. He'd even let her live in the apartment once they got it straightened up. But that was all. He wasn't going to fall for Emma Montgomery, no matter how hard his sister tried.

"It's no problem, Emma," he assured her. "We'll work something out."

Feeling more in control of the situation, he headed toward the car to help. "Hey, Leigh, hold up. The garage apartment is full of junk. Emma will have to stay in the house for a couple of nights."

Emma had been walking along next to him, but now she stopped.

"I'm turning into a real inconvenience," she said. "I feel terrible about this."

They were close enough for Leigh to hear them, and his sister answered before he had the chance.

"Emma, stop being so polite to Nathan. It will make him think even higher of himself than he does already, and none of us wants that. The whole town adores him.

Everyone goes gaga over him, so don't puff up his ego anymore or he's apt to float away."

Nathan nudged his sister. "Hey, remember kiddo, I'm helping you out. Don't bite the hand that's saving your tush."

She rolled her eyes at him, looking more like a six-year-old than a young woman about to graduate from college.

"You know I love you," she said. "But you also have more than your fair share of self-confidence. You don't need Emma telling you how great you are." She fluttered her eyelashes. "You've got the ladies of Honey to do that"

Emma gave him an inquisitive look. "You do?"

Before Nathan could make even a token effort to rescue his reputation, Leigh jumped back in.

"All the ladies in town are besotted with my brother. They chase him relentlessly."

"No, they don't. Not exactly." He ruffled his sister's hair and grabbed a couple of suitcases out of the car.

Leigh turned to Emma. "Trust me. That's exactly what they do. They. Chase. Him."

Nathan shook his head and headed toward the kitchen. There was no sense wasting his breath fighting with Leigh. When she got going, there was nothing to do but hang on for the ride. He could hear the women talking as they followed behind him. His sister discussing him was never a good thing, so he decided to change the subject.

"Emma, you sure you don't want to take the summer off?" Nathan asked. "You could laze around on a beach somewhere."

"I really do need a job this summer. If you don't think—"

"Nathan, you're upsetting Emma," Leigh said. "Stop being rude and assure her that you have a job."

"I already told her I'd work something out." He set down the suitcases and stared at his sister. "In case you've forgotten, up until ten minutes ago, I didn't know you intended on bringing someone home with you. All you told me on the phone last night was that you'd caught a ride with a friend."

If he'd expected Leigh to look contrite, he would have been disappointed. She glared at him.

"Get over that, Nathan. Jeez. It's like ancient history. So I surprised you. Big woo. Now accept that Emma is here and give her a job."

"Leigh, do you always push your brother around like this?" Emma asked.

Nathan pinned Leigh with a direct look. "Yes. She does."

"Oh, you poor baby. I'm so mean to you." Leigh leaned over and gave him another kiss on the cheek. "You adore me, and you know it. If it weren't for me livening up your life, you'd fall into a big pile of computer code and never come out. Admit it— you've been bored while I've been at college, haven't you?"

He pretended to consider her question. "Bored? Have I been bored? My life has been restful while you've been gone."

"Your life will be restful when you're dead, too, but that doesn't make it a good thing."

Nathan laughed. Truthfully, he was glad Leigh was

home. Sure, she was a pain at times, but she also was a lot of fun.

"One of these days, I'm going to move and not give you the forwarding address," he teased as he picked up the suitcases and headed inside the house.

"Won't happen. Now figure out what you're going to do to help Emma."

As he led the way inside the house, he debated which of the two open jobs to offer Emma. One was in personnel, and Emma struck him as the type who would be good with people. The other job was as his assistant His current assistant was on maternity leave, and he was desperate.

"My assistant just had a baby, and I need someone to fill in for a few weeks. Barrett Software is working on an easily customized accounting package for small businesses that we're going to demo in Dallas in six weeks at BizExpo, one of the biggest tech shows in the country. The time frame is kind of tight and the program still has some problems, but if we make it, we'll get a lot of publicity. I really need help keeping everything moving. Sound like something you could do?"

"Of course, Emma can do it," Leigh said with a huff. "She's amazing. Unbelievable. Incredible."

Emma sighed. "Leigh, so help me, if you say I can leap tall buildings in a single bound, I'm heading back to Austin."

"Har-de-har-har," Leigh said. "You two are just a couple of comedians. Here I've gone to all this trouble to help both of you, and you don't even seem to appreciate what I've done."

Nathan winked at Emma. "Do you believe this? She's playing the martyr."

"Doing it well, too," Emma said.

Nathan smiled at her, liking the auburn-haired beauty more and more. He was still looking at Emma when Leigh snorted.

"Fine. Laugh all you want. But there's going to come a day when both of you will thank me for this. Trust me." With that, Leigh flounced up the stairs, carrying one of Emma's suitcases with her.

Emma had come to stand next to him. She smelled like flowers—rich, luxurious flowers, probably due to her shampoo rather than any perfume. The scent was too unintentional to be perfume.

But something about that scent tantalized him more than any expensive perfume ever could.

"Was that a promise or a threat?" Emma asked.

"Sometimes with Leigh, it's hard to tell the difference," he admitted.

EXCERPT: TEXAS RASCALS:
KEEGAN

Wren Matthews took the last of the cranberry-walnut bread from the oven and set the small loaves to cool on the oak sideboard.

The aroma of freshly baked bread and brewing coffee mingled with the hearty scent of beef stew simmering on the stove.

Jaunty strains of Brenda Lee's "Rockin' Around the Christmas Tree" spilled from the radio tuned to a local station so she could catch the weather report, blunting the sound of the winter weather howling outside her door.

Yesterday, it had been a sunny sixty degrees in the Davis Mountains. But this morning, the temperature had plummeted, bringing with it a vibrant electrical storm.

She had finished her Christmas baking just in time to start the evening milking. At the thought of the heavy chores waiting for her, Wren sighed and closed the oven door.

Sometimes the overwhelming responsibility had her thinking of selling the dairy and moving into town, but she simply couldn't bring herself to part with the farm. The modest homestead had been in the Matthews family for three generations. She couldn't bring herself to give up. It was the only life she'd ever known.

Wren washed her hands at the sink and peered out at the cedar trees whipping in the wind. The branches made an eerie scratching noise against the window pane.

It was tough running the place on her own. If only she could find reliable help. Someone to live in the loft apartment over the barn. Someone strong and hard-working. Someone who would keep to himself and leave her be.

But good help was difficult to find in this sparse country where her nearest neighbor, the Markum Ranch, was three miles away.

Perhaps she should advertise for a dairy hand on the social media network for the Rascal, Texas community. For a while, one of the boys from the high school where she taught freshman English, had assisted her.

Then six weeks ago, Jeff had injured his knee playing football, and Wren found herself struggling to meet the dual obligations of teaching and dairy farming all on her own.

Thank heavens for Christmas break. With any luck, she would find someone before school resumed after the new year.

The problem was, she was shy around people she didn't know. Very shy. She required a boarder as intro-verted as herself. Someone who wouldn't want to talk her ear off or become fast friends. Someone who preferred solitude as much as she did.

She turned off the oven, untied her flour-stained, red-and-green apron—with miniature Santa Clauses embroidered across the front—draped it over the cabinet and limped to the back door.

Her old hip injury flared in damp weather, and as much as she hated to give in to the pain, she'd been forced to down two aspirins earlier that evening to ease the ache.

"And now it's time for the six o'clock news," the announcer purred, followed by lead-in music.

Half listening to the broadcast, Wren worked her feet into the yellow rubber boots she'd left drying on newspaper spread over the parquet entryway. While the radio announcer gave a rundown on world and state news, Wren went about her business.

She lifted the heavy down jacket, that had once belonged to her father, from the coat tree in the corner. Shrugged into it. Pulled on the worn leather gloves she took from the pocket.

"The storm moving through the Trans-Pecos is expected to worsen late tonight, plunging temperatures to an all-time record low," the announcer warned. "Bring the pets and plants inside and don't drive if at all possible. This is a night to curl up by the fire with a cup of hot cocoa and a good book."

Now that sounded like Wren's idea of a perfect Friday night.

The icy wind wailed like a mournful banshee around the wooden doorframe, chasing a chill down Wren's spine. If it weren't for the cattle, she'd make sure the door was locked tight, crawl inside her four-poster bed, and take the radio announcer's advice.

But the cows had to be milked, and she was the only one to do it.

Here goes nothing. She rested her hand on the knob at the same time a knock barked at the door.

The sudden noise reverberated in the room like a gunshot blast. Startled, Wren jumped and jerked her hand back. Her stomach churned, and her chest tightened.

Pressing a palm to her mouth, she waited. Prayed it was just a tree branch breaking loose and slamming against the side of the house.

She waited.

The knock came again, denying any fanciful explanations. Someone was at her door.

Who could be visiting in this storm? An eerie sensation lifted the hairs at the nape of her neck.

She didn't get many guests out this far from town— her pastor, some of the little old ladies from her church, one or two teacher friends from the high school, that was about it. In Rascal, she was known as the kooky crippled spinster who lived all alone on her aging dairy farm. And who, at the naive age of nineteen, had once been swindled by a charming con man.

Even now, ten years later, Wren blushed at the memory of Blaine Thomas and her youthful mistake.

She'd been lonely and vulnerable after her parents' deaths. Easy pickings for the likes of smooth-talking Blaine.

He'd used flattery and compliments to make her feel loved when he'd only been after her money. She'd almost lost the farm because of her foolishness, and she'd sworn never again to trust a handsome man.

The knock was bolder, more insistent the third time.

Who could it be? She cocked her head and struggled to muster enough courage to answer the door.

Maybe it was a neighbor in distress. You can't leave someone standing out in this storm, she scolded herself.

And yet, a snake of fear winding around her heart kept her rooted firmly to the floor. Wren placed her hands over her ears. Go away, go away, go away.

"Is anyone home?"

The voice was strong, masculine, demanding. It sharpened Wren's dread.

"I need help."

Too readily, she recalled those terrifying moments eleven years ago. In the wee hours of the morning, she had found herself in a similar situation, dragging her wounded body from door to door, begging people to let her in while her parents' mangled car lay overturned on an icy street. She had practically crawled on her crumpled, bleeding leg, and she'd gone to three houses before a kind, elderly couple had finally opened their door to her.

"Please?"

That single word rent her heart and snuck past her defenses as nothing else would have. What if this man needed her as badly as she'd needed assistance that awful night her parents died?

Resolutely, she put the chain on the door then edged it open a tiny crack. A streak of lightning illuminated the ebony sky, highlighting the figure on her porch.

A hulking stranger loomed in the darkness. The sight of him snatched the air from her lungs. Gasping, Wren slapped a hand over her mouth and took a step backward.

The man was very tall, towering many inches above her own petite five-foot-two-inches, and he was powerfully built, with wide shoulders and large muscular arms. He wore a white felt Stetson, a denim jacket, and worn cowboy boots like most of the ranchers in Presidio County. His dark-blue eyes were deep-set and watchful, his countenance enigmatic and forbidding.

A fresh chill ran through her.

"I'm stranded," he said.

His sharp, clipped speech told her the man wasn't a Texan despite being dressed like a cowboy. A Northerner, she guessed. Chicago, perhaps? The clash in clothing and speech concerned her. He wasn't what he looked like.

The man waited expectantly, his head angled to one side, cold rain blowing into the house around him. Instinct begged her to slam the door and lock it tight against him.

And yet, she hesitated.

"What do you want?" Wren squeaked, her heart pounding, one hand wrapped protectively around the door.

"To come in from the wet and cold."

He spoke in a commanding timbre. His voice reminded Wren of the eerie tone her father had used when he had told ghost stories around the campfire.

"I'm sorry," she shook her head. "I can't help you." She began easing the door closed.

"I understand," he said. "I don't blame you. I wouldn't take a stranger into my home either." Hunching his shoulders, he turned and started down the steps.

Wren slammed the door behind him and slid the deadbolt home. Her pulse, thready and weak, slipped through her veins like water. Her whole body trembled violently, and she sagged against the door to keep from falling over.

Maybe she should call someone. Tell them she was alone with a stranger at the door. But who could she call?

Taking a deep breath, she tried to calm down. "Steady, Wren, just step across the floor to the phone and notify the sheriff. That's all you've got to do."

In the Davis Mountains, a landline was still a necessity. Just a mile outside the Rascal city limits and cell phone reception diminished. This far out and it was nonexistent. She might as well be on the dark side of the moon.

Ugly images kept springing into her mind. Images of that dark, threatening stranger standing outside her window with a sharp knife clutched in his hand, waiting for the opportunity to hurt her.

"Stop it," she hissed under her breath. "Call the sheriff. Now."

Wren put one foot in front of the other, clenching her jaw to block out any other unnecessary visions. Her fingers shook, and she dropped the phone twice before she managed to get it to her ear.

Sterile silence.

The line was dead.

* * *

The stranger slogged through the driving sleet, disappointed but not surprised. Over the course of the last six months, he'd grown accustomed to such treatment. He expected it. But he wasn't opposed to trespassing, especially since the lady's barn appeared so inviting.

A light shone through the barn window, and he could hear cattle lowing and moving restlessly from behind closed doors. It was a dairy farm, he rationalized, the barn was bound to be heated, and he'd slept in worse places. If nothing else, he'd have milk to drink and a dry place to rest his head.

He'd frightened the woman pretty badly. She reminded him of a timid mouse, all wide-eyed and twitchy. She was one of those quiet women that men rarely noticed. Not unattractive, but definitely nothing that snagged interest. She lived alone, he'd figured out, and he doubted that she was brave enough to come into the barn looking for him. This would be as good a place as any to hole up for the night. He'd be gone by morning, and she'd never need to know he'd lingered here.

With a backward glance over his shoulder at the house, the stranger turned and entered the large barn.

The cows greeted him loud and hearty, clearly expecting to be milked. The stranger closed the door behind him and shook off the wet cold. The warm air offered a welcome respite and for the first time in many hours, he felt free to relax his guard.

His gaze fell on a stairwell leading to an overhead loft. Raising a curious eyebrow, he went to investigate, moving past over a dozen stalls of well-fed Holsteins.

He climbed the stairs and pushed open the door into the small sparse room. A cot covered with a worn woolen army blanket sat in one corner, an unplugged space heater rested beside it. There was a sink on the opposite side wall and a toilet cloaked behind a flowered shower curtain. Primitive but functional.

A smile curled his wind-blistered lips.

It would do nicely.

* * *

"Okay, just because the phone is dead doesn't mean he cut the line," Wren said, trying desperately to hearten herself. "It's probably the storm. Remember? The phones went out twice last winter."

Her pathetic reassurances did nothing to comfort her internal quaking. Was the man still prowling out there in the night?

Terrified at the thought, Wren went to every window and made sure they were securely locked, and the curtains drawn. She darted occasional glances into the darkness beyond, knowing that if she looked out to see a face staring back at her, she'd have a heart attack on the spot.

From the kitchen, her radio inanely played on, heedless of her situation. "I Saw Mommy Kissing Santa Claus" flowed into "Grandma Got Run Over by a Reindeer." The rollicking, tongue-in-cheek ditty provided direct contrast to the turmoil from the stranger's mysterious arrival. She thought about turning the radio off, but the prospect of eerie silence was even more unsettling than the merry music.

She interlaced her hands and began to pace, favoring her aching hip. She wondered what to do next. Even through the storm and the song, Wren could hear the cows calling. She glanced at the clock on the wall, saw it was well after six thirty. The ruckus from the barn would only get louder as the cows grew more distended with milk.

"I can't go out there," she muttered.

Wren quivered at the prospect of trekking out into the freezing rain with the interloper on the loose and bit the inside of her cheek.

Perhaps he'd gone.

And perhaps he'd not.

Distressed, she plopped down at the kitchen table and drummed her fingers over the scarred oak. What to do?

A bellowing noise, louder and more insistent than a foghorn, mingled with the shrieking wind and created a nerve-racking cacophony. There was no mistaking Bossie's distinctive clamor. She was the oldest cow in Wren's seventeen-head herd and quite spoiled.

"You can't hide in here all night, Wren," she chided. "The cows have to be milked."

But it can wait, her cautious side argued. Give that dark stranger time to mosey on down the road.

Her sense of responsibility warred with her natural timidity. Finally, Wren struck a bargain with herself. She'd eat supper first, then go milk the cows.

Scraping back her chair on the worn floor, she shrugged out of her coat. She dished up stew into a bowl and retrieved a handful of saltines from the cracker jar. Taking her time, she poured herself a cup of hot tea before settling back in at the table with her meal.

The racket from the barn increased, rising in both tempo and intensity. She blew on a spoonful of stew to cool it and tried her best to tune out the cows' miserable cries, but the food stuck in her throat. Swallowing down the bite, she stared into her bowl.

She couldn't eat. Not now. Not when she was so upset. Not with the cows begging to be milked.

Lightning jumped outside the window. Thunder grumbled, and Wren tightened her grip on the spoon handle, the sounds almost too much to bear.

"And now, the seven o'clock news." The radio crackled. "Worsening weather is the hour's top story," the news announcer said. "Driving rain is rapidly turning to sleet and the temperature has already dropped ten degrees in less than an hour, with tonight's expected low in the single digits."

Wren shivered. There was no way she could keep ignoring the cows. She had to make sure they were warm enough, that the heaters were still working.

"The National Weather Service has issued a severe winter weather advisory. Motorists are cautioned to stay off the roads if at all possible."

Idly, Wren crushed a cracker with the palm of her hand. She couldn't help thinking about that man, out there alone in the wet and cold. Sighing, she pushed her soup bowl across the table. Why she should suddenly feel sorry for the stranger mystified her.

Inclining her head, she dusted the cracker crumbs from her hands. Suddenly, the cows had stopped mooing.

Wren froze. Why?

Her stomach tingled as if she'd eaten a thousand hot

chili peppers and her mouth went dry. Wren got up and turned down the radio. She waited in the middle of the kitchen, head cocked, pulse racing.

Nothing but the wind howling through the trees.

She bit her bottom lip. The cows should be getting louder, not shutting up entirely. This was weird.

Investigate. But Wren stayed rooted to the spot. I'm scared.

Coward.

She fisted her hands. She couldn't stay here all night, cowering in fear. She had to find out what was going on in the barn. No matter how frightening the prospect.

Heaving in deep breaths, in through the nose, out through the mouth three times, Wren bolstered her courage. She donned her coat and gloves once more. She took a small gold key from a rack over the sink and went to the living room to unlock her father's gun cabinet.

She peered at the array of firearms. She knew next to nothing about guns and had only used the .22 on occasion to kill rattlesnakes. Wren wrapped a gloved hand around the wooden stock and lifted the weapon. Locked the cabinet and dropped the key into her pocket.

Could she use the gun on a human being if she had to? Wren gulped. "You can do whatever you have to do to survive." She shook herself. "Now, come on."

Armed with the lightweight .22-caliber semi-automatic, she switched off the safety and headed out the door. Clinging to the barrel, her finger poised near the trigger, Wren struggled through the wind, her hip aching in response to the sorry weather.

She darted furtive looks left and right, but save for the light from the barn, she saw nothing but pitch blackness. A man could be skulking behind any tree, beside any fence, around any corner.

Fear rose high in her throat and heavy down inside her belly. She clutched the gun tighter. Sleet pelted her rain cap and slapped her face with startling cold. She kept her head down, her chin tucked to her chest.

Lightning slashed the dark sky. Thunder rumbled like artillery fire. The air smelled harsh, metallic, the odor of electricity. Every flash and crack punched through her like a missile impact.

Wren couldn't see more than a few feet in front of her, and her teeth chattered in the biting cold. Thick mud clung to her boots, throwing her off balance. She stumbled and trudged forward, fighting the ooze and her escalating terror.

It was a relief to burst into the barn at last, even though she didn't know what she might find there. She kept the gun raised and her back to the wall.

An image from deep down bubbled to the top of her head. A flash of memory. A jagged cut over her eye, blood streaming down her face, her first sharp bite of mortality.

Wren blinked against the brightness, her breath coming in reedy wheezes. What she saw sent her blood pumping swiftly through her eardrums.

The cows were placidly munching oats at their troughs, happily hooked to the milking machines.

What was going on?

Feeling as if she'd fallen into the Twilight Zone head first, Wren battled losing her composure. This was eerie. Unnatural. She cleared her throat and tried to speak, but the words were trapped, unable to get out.

Frantically, she scanned the barn and saw nothing amiss.

The man had to be in here. Who else could have done this?

Sweat flooded her brow and Wren gripped the rifle with all her might. Why would he hook her cows to the milking machines? Did he have some ulterior motive? Or had he simply grown deaf listening to them bellow?

It didn't matter. She'd started down this road and now she had to finish her journey. Gun butt resting against her shoulder, she squinted down the .22's sight. Aimed the weapon and stepped carefully past each stall, one by one.

One, two, three.

Her heart revved faster with each advancing step. Bossie swished her tail and leveled Wren a sassy look.

Four, five, six.

Empty. Empty. Empty.

Seven, eight, nine, ten. The smell of oats lay strong. Hay rustled beneath her boots.

Eleven, twelve, thirteen.

No one.

Fourteen, fifteen, sixteen, seventeen.

All cows accounted for and no stranger in sight.

The hairs on the back of Wren's neck stood at full attention. She rounded the refrigerated milking vat and peeked into every nook and cranny. The nose of the gun preceding her every move.

Nothing.

Slowly, she swung her eyes upward, knowing the stranger must be in the loft.

Probably watching her through a knothole.

Did he have a gun?

That thought deepened her fear. What was she going to do? If she ran back to the house, she wouldn't be able to call the police because the phone was out, and she'd be trapped once more. Giving the stranger the upper hand. At least for the moment, she possessed the advantage.

So what now?

Climb the stairs?

Hang back?

Wait?

There was only one viable option. She had to confront him.

Her knees weakened with the prospect, and Wren swayed on her feet.

"Okay, mister, I know you're up there," she said, surprised by how authoritative she sounded. "I've got a gun trained on the stairs. You better come on down before I start shooting first and asking questions later."

ABOUT THE AUTHORS

Liz Alvin

Liz Alvin has loved reading and writing for as long as she can remember. In fact, she majored in literature at college just so she could spend her days reading great stories. When it came to her own stories, she decided to write romances with happy endings because she's a firm believer in love. She's been married to her own hero for over 30 years. They live in Texas near their adult children and are surrounded by rescue dogs and a rescue cat.

Lori Wilde

Lori Wilde is the New York Times, USA Today and Publishers' Weekly bestselling author of 88 works of romantic fiction. She's a three time Romance Writers' of America RITA finalist and has four times been nominated for Romantic Times Readers' Choice Award. She has won numerous other awards as well.

Her books have been translated into 26 languages, with more than four million copies of her books sold worldwide.

Her breakout novel, *The First Love Cookie Club*, has been optioned for a TV movie.

Lori is a registered nurse with a BSN from Texas

Christian University. She holds a certificate in forensics, and is also a certified yoga instructor.

A fifth generation Texan, Lori lives with her husband, Bill, in the Cutting Horse Capital of the World; where they run Epiphany Orchards, a writing/creativity retreat for the care and enrichment of the artistic soul.

ALSO BY LORI WILDE & LIZ ALVIN

Handsome Devil Series:

Handsome Boss

Handsome Lawman

Handsome Cowboy

ALSO BY Lori Wilde

Texas Rascals Series:

Keegan

Matt

Nick

Kurt

Tucker

Kael

Truman

Brodie

Dan

Rex

Clay

Jonah

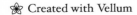

Made in the USA
Monee, IL
23 January 2020